El Malo

K WEBSTER

El Malo
Copyright © 2018 K Webster

Cover Design: All By Design
Photo: Adobe Stock
Editor: Emily A. Lawrence, www.lawrenceediting.com
Formatting: Champagne Book Design

ISBN-13:978-1987684407
ISBN-10:1987684400

Javier Estrada is the king of Mexico.
Evil. Twisted. Psychopathic.
A cruel madman with a killer smile.
And he is my boss.

My duty is to blend in, clean his home, and not make a peep.
I've done my job well for years.
Imbedded myself so deep in his world, he's never going to get me out.

But I am this king's worst nightmare.
Bad men like him took everything away from me.
I will never forget.
He will pay for the sins of many.
I'll just bide my time—watching, waiting, calculating—until the time is right.

When I strike, he won't know what hit him.
The monster who rules Mexico with an iron fist may not bow to anyone…
But I'm not just anyone.

He will bow to me.

Dedication

To my husband—
Thank you for always having my back, honey.

El amor no respeta la ley.

Love doesn't respect the law.

Warning

This book is a dark romance and not recommended for those with triggers.

Prólogo

Rosie Bear

Ten years old...

"Mamá, please," I beg, doing my best to give her the puppy dog eyes she can't ignore. Mamá may be hard around the edges, but she's soft for me. My grandmother says it's because Papá went to prison. Mamá has to be both a good mother and father to me. She's firm when she needs to be but soft too. Always soft for me.

"I need to get ready for work," she tries, but her dark brown eyes twinkle.

"Work isn't for three more hours." I scrunch my nose and pout. Plenty of time to go to Ciudad Juárez to my favorite restaurant just across the border.

She purses her lips and turns off the iron. My mother takes pride in ironing her uniforms she wears for the motel she works at. I love how pretty she looks before she leaves. The black dress hugs her curvy body and her white collar is always crisp. I notice men and women alike admiring my mother. It makes me proud because she's so beautiful.

"Fine, *mija*," she says, giving in. "Grab a jacket in case it gets chilly in the restaurant."

"Yay!" I squeal and throw myself into her arms. She smells heavenly like lavender and *her*. There's just a fragrance to her that makes her unique.

Thirty minutes later and we're driving over the border into Mexico. We make this trip often and as long as we go during the day, we don't run into any issues. Once, Mamá forgot to bring a second identification card and we got held up on our way back in. But Mamá always smiles real big and pretty to get her way. I try to smile big and pretty like her too.

"They're so busy," she complains as she circles the parking lot for a spot. "I hope the wait isn't too long. I don't want to be late for work."

I frown, hoping we can get right in. Ana, the old woman who works the front counter, usually finds a place for us, though. I'll give her one of the bracelets I made for my friend Amanda. Maybe she'll find some chairs in the back for us to sit at.

"Ah, the luck!" Mamá cries out as a big truck backs out of a spot. I hoot in excitement as we pull in right in front of the building.

She calls after me when I burst from the car and run inside. As soon as I open the door, the spices fill my nose and my stomach grumbles. This is my favorite place. I love everything they make and could eat here every day. Mamá says if she eats here every day her butt will be bigger than Texas where we live. I just giggle, trying to imagine a butt that big.

"Dearest Rosa!" Ana calls out and opens her arms for a hug. I run into her arms and squeeze the woman who reminds me much of my grandmother. "How are you today?"

I beam up at her. "Great! Mamá thinks we'll have to wait." I tug a bracelet from my pocket and tie it around her old, wrinkly wrist. "But maybe you could find us a table," I whisper.

She narrows her eyes as she inspects the bracelet. "You sure know how to drive a hard bargain," she says, the corners of her eyes crinkling. "There's a table in the kitchen you two can sit at. I'll make sure Miguel cooks you up something special today."

"Thanks, Ana," Mamá tells her and tugs at my ponytail. "You're spoiled, *mija*."

I giggle as we follow Ana toward the back. She gets us settled at the dinky table in the corner. It's exciting to be in the kitchen and watch the guys cook. Miguel is as old as Ana but real big and fat. I bet that's because he eats all the good foods he makes. Maybe he'll be as big as Mexico if he keeps eating like that.

"What are you laughing about?" Mamá asks.

I point at Miguel. "Look at his belly, Mamá!"

"Shhhh," she chides. "Don't be rude, Rosie Bear. That's not nice."

Pouting, I scan the kitchen, hoping to see something exciting. My eyes land on a man wearing a blue bandana. It reminds me of the pictures of my father. The pictures my mother only lets me see on occasion. Papá has tattoos on his neck and face like the man beside Miguel. Both he and my father have the same hard stares. I wonder if the man knows Papá. Maybe they were in the same gang? I'm about to open my mouth to ask when the man raises his voice at Miguel.

More men, dressed just like the man pour in through the back door. They all carry shiny guns and knives.

"You leave my restaurant!" Ana yells and points out the back door.

Mamá turns and lets out a garbled sound. She stands and presses her butt against me, squishing me against the wall.

"¡Este hijo de puta me debe dinero!" the scariest man yells at Miguel. *This motherfucker owes me money!*

Miguel mutters something about not having it. I blink, trying to see past my mother to watch.

Pop! Pop! Pop!

Explosive gunfire shatters the air and Mamá pushes me to the floor, her body covering mine in a protective way. More shots fire, over and over again, and glass breaks all around the kitchen. I scream at the top of my lungs, overcome with terror. Mamá pushes her hand against my mouth, but her hand is wet.

Tears spill from my eyes and I try to hide from the scary men. They're not like Papá. Papá would never shoot up my favorite restaurant. Papá would never yell at a nice cook like Miguel. I may not remember Papá, but I feel this in my heart.

"My sweet Rosie Bear," Mamá whispers against my hair, her hand sliding from my mouth. "Be a good girl. I love you."

I can hear screams within the restaurant but aside from some shuffling, the kitchen is quiet. Those bad men finally left.

"Mamá," I whisper. "They're gone."

But Mamá is so protective, she keeps me smashed to the floor under her weight. Maybe her butt *is* going to be the size of Texas soon because she is heavy.

"Mamá!" I cry out. "Move, Mamá!"

She doesn't move. She doesn't speak. I squirm out from beneath her and my eyes land on Ana. She's on the ground, a pool of blood around her body. Her arm lies twisted out in front of her, my bracelet I gave her soaking up blood. Everything is broken around me.

"Mamá!" I scream. "They hurt Ana!"

Mamá doesn't care. She's sleeping and I need her to be awake. I shove her over onto her back.

Blood.

Blood.

Blood.

No, Mamá, no.

"No!" I wail. "No!"

Bright red blooms of blood cover her shirt like big roses in several spots. She's been shot all over her chest. Her eyes that always twinkle with delight are open but dulled. Mamá's mouth is parted and unmoving.

My mother is not dead.

She is not dead.

"Mamá!"

She. Is. Not. Dead.

Capítulo Uno

Rosa

Present...

"**Y**our corners are messy," I chide as I unfold the sheet and show my newest charge how to properly fold the linens. "Like this, Araceli."

Araceli, an eighteen-year-old Mexican woman, watches with wide eyes as I show her. With time, she'll learn how things run around here. I run a tight ship and they all must stay on their toes to keep up with my level of perfection.

I'm borderline OCD when it comes to this house.

No dust. No crinkles. No mess.

It must remain as clean as possible, for who lives within it is far from so.

"Let me try," she says, determination in her tone. I love the fierce woman who lives beneath the unsureness and slight awkwardness. Araceli reminds me of myself ten years ago when I was her age.

I've grown into this hard, formidable woman.

Strength hidden behind a soft, sweet, compliant package.

1

I watch her fold the sheet, my eyes scrutinizing her work for errors. She flawlessly folds it and pride surges within me. "Excellent work, *querida*."

She beams under my praise as I don't give it often. Araceli has been working in the Estrada home for three weeks now and this is the first real compliment I've given her. When you work at a place like this, there's no room for vulnerability and softness. You must always be striving for perfection and watching for danger.

"Run along and make the beds."

Her dark brows scrunch together. "*¿Señor* Estrada?"

All warm thoughts leak from my body as cold settles in my bones. I lift my chin and pierce her with an icy stare. "No. Since when do you ever make *Señor* Estrada's bed?"

She cowers under my biting words. "Never."

"Never," I agree. "Never. Only I am to be trusted in his room. I'll make his bed and that is the end of this conversation."

Her bottom lip quivers as though I've struck her. True, I may have a soft spot for little Araceli, but I can't let her get too comfortable here. None of my ladies are. It's unsafe. We must always be on guard, stay out of the way, and keep the house looking impeccable.

"I'm sorry, Rosa," she murmurs.

I don't correct her for not calling me *Señorita* Delgado. She's upset and I'll allow it this once. "Run along," I snip.

Once she's gone, I pick up the folded sheet and bring it to my nose. My heart clenches when I inhale the scent of lavender and detergent. I'd never realized the smell I associated with my mother was laundry detergent. And now, because of my job, I smell her every day. Each second of each day is a reminder of what I lost.

My eyes prickle, but tears don't form. I've spent almost twenty years learning to harden my heart and block my emotions. The last four, I've specifically honed that skill. I've become like them. A jaguar stalking my prey. I'm good. Very good. None of them, especially him, suspect a thing.

And when the time is right, I'll bring down every last one of them.

Until then, I lie in wait. Crouched low in the grass. My mouth watering and my claws sharp. Javier Estrada, the leader of El Malo, will be ripped to shreds by the time I'm done with him.

Patience is my friend.

My fuel.

My motherfucking sustenance.

Clearing my head with a slight shake, I carry the sheet to the closet. Once I've neatly tucked it inside, I smooth my palms over my crisp black uniform and stride through the massive almost eighteen-thousand-square-foot seaside mansion. All the windows are open facing the Pacific Ocean. The breeze is warm and it fills my lungs with a sense of purpose. I'm silent, my shoes not even making a squeak as I slip through the house. I check for dust on picture frames along the way. Yolanda and Silvia tend to get starry-eyed around the men at times and slack off. I have to stay on those two. Both women are too beautiful for their own good. One day, their beauty will get them hurt.

I stop in front of a giant mirror in the hallway and stare at my reflection. I study the glass for smears but really, I look at myself. I look at *her*. The spitting image of my mother. Wide brown eyes. Dark, almost black, sculpted brows. Full, naturally pink lips. My mocha brown hair that normally hangs in loose waves halfway down my back is pulled tight into a bun at the base of my neck. At work, I remain plain and hidden. I don't want any attention on myself whatsoever. The diamond stud earrings that belonged to my mother are the only shiny piece of me. They catch the light and sparkle in my reflection.

Blood.

Blood.

So much blood.

I blink away the memory of myself sitting on the bathroom floor of my grandmother's house scrubbing my mother's bloody earrings with a toothbrush. Every day for weeks, I'd scrub at those earrings. Grandmother said the blood was long gone, but I could sense it there. I wasn't satisfied until I'd cleaned them every day for a month.

Sometimes I still wonder about the blood.

Giggles resound from a nearby room and I jolt. The girls. I storm down the hallway, a scowl on my face. As soon as I enter Marco Antonio's room, Javier's second-in-command, I discover Yolanda and Silvia. Neither of them is working. No, they are tossing a pair of his boxer briefs at one another. Such foolish behavior could get them killed.

"¡Suficiente!" *Enough!* I snap as I rush over and tear the underwear from Silvia's grip.

Yolanda starts laughing and my blood boils with the blatant disrespect.

"I suggest you two separate and do your jobs. I'm

writing you both up over this. That makes two for each of you now. You know, one more and you're gone," I warn.

They both lose their smiles and hang their heads. On one hand, I feel guilty for taking away such a small pleasure as giggling over a man's boxers. But he's not just any man. Marco Antonio is vicious and cruel. I've had to clean up his bloodshed more than I'd like to remember. Half of his clothes end up in the trash because some stains simply don't come out. Violence is a stain that imbeds in the fibers and never lets go.

I wave them away and they run off, their heels clacking the wood floors in their wake. No matter what I try to impress upon them, they don't listen. It will be their end one day. I hate that for them. I hate that these young girls grew up in the ravished parts of Guerrero, Mexico, and think this place is their happily ever after. That they feel safe here. They aren't safe anywhere. Acapulco isn't what it used to be in the '50s and '60s when The Kennedys and Frank Sinatra would vacation here. Back then, it was family oriented and a true attraction for tourists.

Now, just beyond the mansions that line the beaches and the fancy resorts is a city overrun by corruption and out of control violence. Violence that is fed morsel by morsel by none other than my boss.

Javier Estrada.

I quickly fold Marco Antonio's boxers and place them in his drawer. His weapons are stuffed in the strangest places. I never touch them, but I catalogue them in my head. If I ever need an out, it's in Marco Antonio's room I'll find that out. He's got an arsenal ready. And just like he always wants to be quick to annihilate if things go south and quick, so do I.

The last thing I need is for young, silly girls to ruin that for me. As of today, I'll add his room to the ones they aren't allowed to touch.

Booming voices jerk me from my inner thoughts and I hurry from his room. Javier and his men have arrived home from some business in the city. Usually, someone comes back injured or wearing the blood of someone they've injured. Always, I'm stuck cleaning up after their mini wars they have each day.

Quickly, I rush through the hallways to peek in at them. Marco Antonio, Arturo, and Alejandro are gathered around Javier's favorite leather chair in the living room. I can't see him, just the backs of his men, but I sense him. Javier is evil personified. Death and corruption and sadism all rolled into one magnificent package.

I try not to think about that part of him. The part that has my girls' cheeks turning pink any time he glances at them. Javier is handsome. Charismatic even. But behind his wide, flirtatious grins are hate and fury and madness. I wish I could throttle each of my girls and remind them we are in the lion's den. They're simply meat for him to bite into if he gets hungry.

I, however, am not meat.

I am a worthy adversary.

He just doesn't know it yet.

"Dissension is key," Javier's rugged, masculine voice rumbles. It always seems to rattle my nerves. It coils in the pit of my belly like a snake. No matter how hard I try not to let him affect me, he does. When I look at Javier, I see the monsters who killed my mother and Ana and Miguel. I hate him as much as I hate the ones who were actually responsible.

"What does that mean?" Alejandro asks. He's the runt of the group. Massive and muscular being that he was an ex-MMA fighter, but dumber than a box of rocks.

Marco Antonio grunts. "You have a phone. Google it, asswipe."

Alejandro shoves him, but Marco Antonio is twice as solid. Older and meaner. He doesn't budge and that only serves to piss Alejandro off even more.

"It means," Javier interrupts, always so patient with his young goon, "we'll continue to encourage the dissension among rival gangs and cartels. Worm our way into each clan. El Malo will be like a disease. We'll slowly infect the entire region. One man at a time. And when they're all relying on us for their next paycheck and meal, we'll cut off the dead weight. Rein in the strong and moldable. These motherfuckers will live and breathe El Malo. I will rule Guerrero with an iron fist."

"Fuck yeah," Arturo agrees. He's closer to Marco Antonio's age. Early thirties. He's leaner than the other two goons, but I've seen him in hand-to-hand combat on the estate. Arturo's hands are lethal. He can kill a man within seconds simply from using his bare hands.

I'm standing behind one of the massive stone pillars at the edge of the living room. I want to edge closer since they are distracted, but I know that won't do. Instead, I lean my ear out and listen for their plans.

"Tomorrow, we'll go see Mayor Velez. I have some favors I need to call in," Javier growls.

I know what he means by favors. I've worked here for four years and favors mean he has information on a man and plans to blackmail him. I take mental note of the name.

The scent of candy apple and tobacco permeates my senses. I can smell Javier coming from a mile away because of his favorite vice. Where most men in powerful positions smoke the fat cigars you have to cut and prepare, Javier smokes the "little cigars." And not just regular ones but the candy apple flavored ones. It's almost laughable. In America, the media gets their panties in a wad complaining about how those little cigars appeal to minors because they taste and smell like candy.

If they only knew.

One of the biggest monsters in Mexico has a hard-on for them.

A rare smile tilts my lips up. Would Javier change his smoking habits if he knew a bunch of fifteen-year-olds in the US smoke the same crap he does just to seem cool? Something tells me he'd be annoyed by that fact. And that makes me smile.

The men continue hashing out details and when I realize the conversation is over, I slip away down another hallway.

I'm always watching and listening, Estrada.

And one day, I'm going to bring your candy apple ass down.

Capítulo Dos

Rosa

I pull my ball cap low on my brow as I trot along the street toward the Pueblo Viejo hotel. It's been around since the beginning of time and I don't think they've painted since. The building was once white but now each time a breeze rolls in from the ocean, old flecks of the paint scatter in the wind. The place is in shambles.

But it serves my purpose.

I sneak in a side door and begin looking under door-mats. The room varies from time to time, although the location remains the same. Each Saturday, I meet my "father." Not David Daza, my real father. No, I meet Michael Stiner. Stiner and I go way back. He's my only friend in this godforsaken world. The only person who knows the real me.

I finally lift a mat that holds a dirty brass key. This hotel is so old it doesn't have fancy key cards like most newer hotels. They're old-fashioned and dirty keys are their thing. I quickly push the key into the hole and step into the room that reeks of stale cigarette smoke and mildew. Michael has opened the sliding glass door to let in some ocean breeze, but it doesn't help. Just stirs up the dust and lifts the smell into the air. I don't tell him this. Not that he'd listen anyway.

He's standing in front of the open doorway, staring out at the ocean past the busy street. Michael is taller than my five-foot-six frame by four or five inches. Over the years, his once fit body has grown pudgy, especially his stomach. And sandy-blond hair, he used to style in a frat boy way, is now thinned out and he combs it over to hide the fact he's losing hair. But his looks mean nothing to me. It's his heart. I know, deep down, he loves me, even if he never actually says the words.

"Hey," I mutter as I come up behind him and hug him. I inhale his scent. The lingering smell of greasy French fries makes my stomach grumble. The house cook, Leticia, makes things Javier approves of. Lots of fresh fish and vegetables. Because our fearless leader is obsessed with his physique, the rest of us suffer. No fried foods or sweets. I get to indulge once a week, on my day off, with my quasi boyfriend.

"Hey, babe," he says, his hand patting mine that now rests on his protruding stomach. "How are you doing?"

I let out a heavy sigh. "Been better. Save me any fries?"

He grunts. "Nah, they were shit anyway."

I try not to pout because I'd eat moldy fries at this point. Instead, I pull away. He turns in my arms and smiles at me. Michael has a boyish look about him that's charming. I fell for his smile years ago.

My stomach growls and I hope we can at least grab me a bite to eat before we get down to business. Michael has other plans. His mouth crashes to mine and he kisses me. I can taste the onions from his burger and it's almost enough to have me recoiling. But then his fingers tenderly slide into my hair and I melt against him. I want the kiss and affection to last longer because I'm feeling emotionally brittle this week, but we're already moving past that as he pulls away my hat and starts tugging at my T-shirt.

"I missed you," I tell him as I raise my arms.

He tears off the shirt and sends it hurtling to the filthy floor. I try not to cringe and think about what sort of yuck I'll collect on my clothes. He tugs at my bra hook, but after a few seconds of fumbling, I do it for him. I toss my bra on the dresser as he works on the buttons of my jeans. Soon I'm naked and he drops his pants to his ankles. He pushes his white briefs down his thighs and they stop at his knees.

"Bend over," he orders, his voice rough as he strokes himself hard.

Today, of all days, I need him on top of me and kissing my mouth. The memory of my mother's death is plaguing my every thought. I want to ask him of these things but instead, I let him bend me over the bed. I hear the tear of the foil packet behind me and then his shirt tickles my ass as his dick pokes against me. This is his new thing. Fucking me with his shirt on. Another item on a long list of stuff that bothers me. I don't care if he's gained weight. I just crave that skin-to-skin connection.

"Michael," I beg, fisting the worn duvet.

He pushes inside me and real tears spring to my eyes. God, it's only been a week of no contact and I didn't realize how much I missed this. With his hands digging into my hips, he ruts against me. I don't even care if I don't get off. I can tell it's one of those days. Something is equally bothering him and I'll take one for the team.

One, two, three, four, five, six.

On the seventh pound into me, he comes with a groan. His thrusting slows. I stare at the floral pattern on the bed as he pulls out of me and disappears into the bathroom to deposit the condom. My legs start to shake so I rise to my feet and quickly pick up my panties from the floor. I'm just stepping into them when he waltzes out of the bathroom. His flaccid cock shrinks back up and hides beneath his shirt, as though it's done for today.

He walks past me and dresses quickly. I do the same and then sit down on the bed. My brows furrow together when he rummages around in his bag. He eventually produces a tape recorder and sits in the desk chair.

"Okay, tell me everything," he instructs.

I swallow down my emotions and let the anger that's guided me through the years flood back into place. For it was the anger that had me getting straight As in school. The anger that got me into the academy. The anger that landed me in a well-sought after position with the CIA.

Agent Daza.

Working undercover as Rosa Delgado.

I'd scoffed when they gave me the name Rosa. It's my real name. But my superiors, including Agent Michael Stiner, assured me that having the same first name would be more believable because I'd always answer to it.

I let out a steady breath and launch into every minute detail of each conversation over the past week since I saw Michael last. I give him descriptions of men who have visited the estate. Names. Locations. Times. The CIA is gaining intelligence at this point. No raids or shutdowns. The chaos that is Guerrero isn't something that can be stopped with a task force. It's too out of control. They're trying to learn the infrastructure of El Malo and their rivals. Picking them apart and dissecting how they work. Then, once they've gained enough information, they'll infiltrate the groups when they're better equipped to do so.

My eyes flit out to the ocean as I talk. It's a bright sunny day, but the high winds tell me a tropical storm could be headed our way. Tropical storms mean prep work to the outside of the Estrada estate. I begin to fret over the newly cleaned patio furniture and cushions. If the wind is this bad now, the cushions are probably scattered out to sea by now. Nobody but me thinks about these things. Nobody but me—

"Rosa."

I blink away my daze and meet Michael's blue-eyed stare. He wears a disapproving frown that makes my stomach hollow out. Tears threaten and I blink them away.

"What's wrong?" he questions, his voice soft.

"Nothing," I lie.

His nostrils flare and I know he can see right past it. "Do I need to pull you out of there?"

I jerk to my feet. "W-What? No! I've been working my ass off for four years, Michael. Four years."

He lets out a heavy sigh. "Everyone at Langley is asking about you. The information is solid, but Stokes is worried you've been under too long."

"No," I argue. "Give me a psyche eval. Do whatever you need to do to make Stokes happy. I'm fine. I swear. It's just been a long week cleaning dust out of every crevice of a giant house that's got me feeling wacky." I walk over to him and rest my hands on his shoulders. He turns off the recorder and looks up at me. "I swear I'm fine. I just miss you. This and us."

He opens his mouth like he wants to say something but then closes it. Guilt flashes in his eyes, which makes me feel uneasy. "Okay, babe. I trust you."

I settle in his lap and he hugs me to him while he types things into his phone one-handed. Safe in my friend's arms, I let my eyes flutter closed. I'm always on edge at the Estrada estate. My guard is never fully down. With Michael, I can relax.

"When we finally bring this operation down and I get to come home, maybe we can see about getting a place together," I murmur.

He stiffens. Michael always acts squeamish any time I suggest we further our relationship. Today is no different. "We'll see, Rosa. We'll see."

This time, I let the tear escape. It rolls down my cheek and clings to my jaw, refusing to jump off and soak his shirt.

No one will ever know the heartache I keep locked deep inside.

No one.

After an afternoon of quiet cuddles and one more quick fuck not much different than the other one, I finally leave. Saturday may be my day off, but I still reside at the Estrada home. And nobody wants to be out after dark in the heart of the city, not even a heavily trained CIA operative. I'm a woman, therefore I'm seen as an easy target. And while I may be able to kick a lot of men's asses, I'm no good against a spray of bullets or a gang of guys. What I have between my legs is often more sought after than guns or weapons.

Knowing the streets and the violence that ensues there, I carry a knife with me and leave my purse at home. With my hair tucked into my hat and dressed in an oversized T-shirt and baggy jeans, I avoid most attention. I keep my head down and my feet moving. Wind whips at my face and my hat goes flying off in a gust. I groan when I twist to see it halfway down the street. My dark locks dance in the wind like a flag calling everyone around me to look.

And boy do they look.

It's times like these I wish it were okay for Michael to walk me back. But we can't compromise him like that. We can't compromise either of us. So, I go at it alone. Even now as I see a guy twice my size making a beeline my way. Experience has taught me that you don't wait to see if the local is just asking for directions.

No…you run.

I burst down the street running as fast as I can. Each night, I sneak off to Javier's gym and run for hours on his treadmill. Long after everyone goes to sleep. It pays off for times like these. I can hear the guy grunting not far behind me, but he already sounds winded. There's a trail that will take me up the side through a thicket of trees to the Estrada estate coming up. I can get off the main road and lose this asshole there. As soon as I see the small gap of trees indicating a trail, I dart off in that direction.

A shot pops off and ricochets off a tree near me. I squeak out in surprise, making sure to duck as I charge along the trail.

Pop! Pop!

I don't know why this guy is shooting at me, but I'll be damned if I die from some coke head jerkoff. Not when I've put this much time into avenging my mother.

That's what I'm doing after all.

Bringing down all the Mexican monsters who prey on the innocent and destroy lives.

I'll bring every last one of them down.

Including Javier. Especially Javier.

I reach into my pocket and pull out my knife. Once I have it flipped open and in my grip, I twist and bend, ready for my attacker. It catches him off guard to see me face off with him. That one small falter is the chance I take. With a hard jab of my fist to his throat, I immobilize him. Another shot pops off and it reminds me to free him of his gun. I raise my arm and then whack it into his. He loses his grip and it falls into the grass with a thud.

Thwap.

Thwap.

Thwap.

I pierce his gut with my knife three quick times. In this world, it's kill or be killed. I know this. Michael knows this. The entire CIA knows this. Hell, even Javier and his men know this. Nobody thinks twice when you kill someone defending yourself.

He groans and holds his stomach as he falls to his knees. I grab a fistful of his greasy hair and bring my knee into his chin. Several of his teeth crack from his gums and tumble from his lips. He falls back and I kick the gun away from him. I'm just about to turn and haul ass out of there when he throws a rock at me, hitting me in the forehead.

Stars glitter in my vision and I stumble backward. I lose my footing and tumble down a hill, whacking a few trees along the way. When I finally crash against a big rock and my tooth cuts into my lip, I let out a groan and clutch my now smarting rib. I wait for the guy to come after me, but I don't hear a sound. After several moments, I pick myself up off the ground and climb back up the slope. As soon as I reach his body, I realize he's dead. The asshole had enough left in him to lob that rock at me but that was it. I don't bother concealing the body. Instead, I limp all the way back to my residence. There's a gate that allows access into the property and I quickly key in the code. It slides open with a whine and I rush onto the safety of Estrada's land. It's getting dark and I pray no one will notice. The last thing I need are my girls fussing over me and asking questions.

I open the front door and then push it closed behind me. The house is silent, so I creep through the kitchen to the stairwell that leads to the servants' quarters. All five house servants sleep upstairs above the kitchen. I don't bother with the kitchen lights and walk quietly past. I'm watching my feet as I reach the stairs and cry out when I run into something.

The smell.

It hits me like a sucker punch to the gut.

Candy apples.

"Rosa Delgado." My name on his lips is like when a lion growls out a warning. Low and deadly. Threatening.

I freeze and back up, my head bowed in respect. This job has been successful for me because I play by the rules. Avert my eyes, keep my mouth shut, and avoid a faceoff with him at all costs. The house servants are just part of the background to a spoiled asshole like him. Every bit as mundane to him as the pictures decorating the walls. I've tried to remain off Javier's radar, although sometimes I catch his gaze lingering on me whenever I'm in the room. Curious and intense. The last thing I need is him to stare a little too long. He may not like what he finds.

"*Señor* Estrada," I greet, my voice a submissive whisper. With my head bowed, I'm stuck staring at his stomach. His white T-shirt is clean and flawless as it stretches over his ripped muscles. He wears dark, baggy jeans and his white tennis shoes are in perfect shape. Javier may be scum of this earth, but he dresses impeccably. Even I can appreciate that in a person.

"Where are you off to in such a hurry, *preciosa*?" *Precious.* His finger slides beneath my chin as he tilts my head up.

I'm forced to stare into his nearly black eyes. Eyes that reflect the monster who lives within. The same violence dances in his gaze that did in the men who shot my mother. They're all the same. Sick. Fucking horrible.

Swallowing down my rage, I start to reply, but then he glowers at me. His strong fingers curl around my jaw, locking me into place as he swats the kitchen light on. I squint against the brightness. Up close, he's even more frightening. It's like I can see into the black hole of his soul. It's terrifying and empty.

"What happened to you?" he demands, his voice trembling with anger.

I wince at his tone and try to avert my gaze. His fingers bite into me, causing me to dart them back his way. "I, uh, was visiting my father. On the way back, I was attacked."

His black eyebrows furl together and his nostrils flare. "Do you know who it was? I will kill him for hurting my property."

I want to slap his hand away and spit in his face. I'm not his property. But I know my place and my job. I know my reason for being here. I'm calm because I have to be. It's what I was trained for.

"Some random guy. I, uh, I got away." I hate that I'm stammering, and that maybe he can sense my fear.

He releases me and steps aside. I dart toward the stairs, but he stops me, a strong hand tightening around my bicep. "I didn't say you could leave." He lets go of me after a beat of silence.

I try not to tremble, and nod. Turning, I find him walking over to the sink. He wets a paper towel and then motions for me to come his way. My heart is racing in my chest and I just want to leave his presence so I can take a hot shower. I want to curl up at the bottom and cry my eyes out. Today is not my day. Instead, I walk over to him and lift my chin. Our eyes meet and I study him up close. It's not a requirement of the job, but I pretend for a second that it is. His nearly black eyes have slivers of light brown in them. Like tiny cracks trying to let light protrude through them. Now, that, is almost laughable.

Javier Estrada is the darkest of dark.

I've seen what he can do.

Over and over and over again.

He's every bit as lethal as his goons. Probably more so. I know his fist alone can break bones. I've heard them crunch. I've cleaned up the blood those punches have left behind.

With his eyes locked on mine, he dabs at the cut on

my lip. I can tell I'll have a bruise on my forehead where the rock hit me. All the scratches on my face and arms from my tumble will heal within a few days. I'm fine. I certainly don't need the cartel king seeing to my wounds.

"I was just coming to speak with you," he murmurs, his eyes narrowing as he studies my reaction.

"Oh?" I give him none. I know this game.

His shoulders relax. "I'm having a party for my father and his family. They're flying in from Puerto Vallarta in a couple of weeks. I want the house immaculate and ready for entertaining." He plucks a leaf that's stuck in my messy hair and pulls it away, causing me to shiver. I wait to see if he'll drop it on the floor, but he keeps it in his hand. If anything, Javier Estrada is clean.

"*Sí, señor.*"

He smirks, a dimple forming on his right cheek. "Good. So compliant."

I bristle at his words. "Have Arturo let me know of any specifics." My brow lifts slightly as if to say, *Why didn't you send him to ask me these things in the first place?*

Irritation flits over his features, stealing the dimple. It makes me want to cheer for getting under his skin. But then I remember who he is. Antagonizing Javier Estrada is not on my list of job duties according to the Central Intelligence Agency.

Blending in.

Staying quiet.

Taking notes.

That is my job.

"*Buenas noches, señor,*" I utter before slipping away.

He doesn't reply...not that I stick around to hear it anyway.

Capítulo Tres

Rosa

My nerves are on edge. It's been a week since my run-in with Javier, but I've been unsettled ever since. Each time I think he'll stop me and narrow his gaze on me, he doesn't. He goes about his very busy days. In and out of the estate. Always on the phone. I've learned that he's beefing up security for his father Yoet and Yoet's wife Tania's arrival, which means they're bringing more bodyguards into his home. All of them are professional, not like the thugs in the city. There are a few, though, with wandering eyes.

Like the one named Julio. He's tall and strong like the rest but something in his eyes gives me the creeps. I'll certainly have my eyes on that one.

Clearing my head, I quickly tie my hair into a bun and look at my reflection. A faint yellow bruise remains on my forehead, but the cut on my lip has since healed. I'm fairly back to normal, which I'm glad for. Tomorrow I'll see Michael and the last thing I need is for him to worry over my safety and pull me out. I've come too far to be pulled out now.

I exit my room and head to meet with my staff to go

over some tasks. Our time is running out and we have much to do. In the servant's quarters, it's broken into two rooms. Since I am the head maid, I have my own room. The other four share one. Loud music plays on the stereo. Yolanda. I've told her a million times to keep it down, but she's nineteen, beautiful, and has a bit of a rebellious streak. I fear for her future the most. I'm about to get on to her but when I walk in, I can't help but smile, which is rare these days.

Yolanda has a hold of Leticia's hands—disfigured from arthritis—and they're dancing. The nearly eighty-year-old woman whose face is lined with heavy wrinkles and is always frowning is laughing. My heart squeezes in my chest. Silvia and Araceli are also dancing. Both giggling at Yolanda's over the top theatrics.

These women are the closest thing to family I have. I know I run a tight ship, but the more time I spend here, the more I realize I'll do whatever it takes to protect them. There have been many sad, lonely nights that Leticia would let me put my head in her lap as she'd stroke my hair. Just like my grandmother used to do. I would silently cry, soaking her lap, and she would just hum unfamiliar songs to me. Those days are fewer the longer I am here, but they still come. Like last Saturday. After my altercation and then subsequent run-in with Javier, I was upset and rattled. Leticia sensed it. Cuddled me and told me to let go of all the pain. Of course I didn't, but in that moment I was free.

I shake away the feelings in my tender heart and clear my throat. Araceli squeaks and rushes to turn off the radio. They are all dressed in their uniforms, but Yolanda doesn't have makeup on yet and the two younger women haven't put up their hair. Leticia is ready, though.

"*Buenos días, señoritas,*" I say, my voice sharper than I intend.

Araceli flinches at my tone. I know I've become hard and sometimes I wish I could be softer for them, but it's too difficult to be all the parts of me. Some of those gentler aspects of myself are forced into the shadows.

"We have a busy day ahead of us. Arturo wants the second floor fitted with new décor that's been brought in. As of last night, the boxes were all stacked up in the hallways. I've already washed the new bedding for those rooms. We'll need to put most of our efforts into making those rooms extra special for *Señor* Estrada's father."

"Emiliano will be coming?" Leticia asks, her features warm. "He must be three now?"

I blink at her in confusion. There are a lot of things I may know, but I can't remember Yoet and Tania's son's age. Last time he'd been at the estate, he was an infant. "Um, I'm not sure."

Leticia beams. "I will make sure I've prepared plenty to eat for the little one. I'll ask Arturo for any dietary restrictions." A sigh escapes her. "I miss my grandchildren. They've moved out of Guerrero and I don't see them as often. What a joy it will be to have little Emiliano here."

I force a smile. Having a child in a murderer's lair isn't exactly exciting news to me. It makes my already brittle nerves crack and fray. I'd hate to have to call in backup to help a toddler if things go sour. And I know myself, the innocent come first. Over this job, over everything. I let out a heavy sigh. I hope it doesn't come to that.

"Will Tania be here?" Yolanda asks as she smears on her blood-red lipstick.

I choose my battles carefully with her. Today I'm not going to argue over her outrageous lip shade.

"She is Javier's stepmother, so I assume so," I say with a huff.

Silvia snickers. "She's younger than Javier. Do you think they've ever had sex? What if Emiliano is not Yoet's but his son's instead. Oh, the drama!"

"¡Cállate!" I hiss. "You have been watching too many telenovelas. And you will address him as *Señor* Estrada. *Señor* Estrada loves his father dearly. He would never hurt him."

The last thing I need is for these young women to gossip themselves into getting hurt. Talk like this, if heard by the wrong person, could end badly.

"You want all of us working on the second floor?" Araceli asks, her voice mousy. Today she's got her thick hair pulled into a high ponytail that seems to accentuate her big brown eyes. Even with no makeup, she's the most beautiful woman in the room.

"Leticia will prepare meals per usual and I'll maintain the rest of the home. But, yes, I want the three of you working up there. Please divide up," I snip, pointing at Silvia and Yolanda. "We don't have time for games. There is too much to do."

Both women nod.

"If you don't have any questions, you're free to get to work. Stay away from the men in the house. There are new ones and they don't appear to be trustworthy," I warn, my heart rate quickening.

Yolanda and Silvia giggle.

"Especially you two. Tomorrow, on your day off, you can flirt to your heart's content outside of this estate.

Although, I must warn you, the violence is getting to be ridiculous," I grumble.

Yolanda puffs out her chest and arches a brow. "My brother's best friend comes and gets us. He has guns, so we're always safe. We've been taking Araceli with us."

Pride surges through me. For as careless as Yolanda is sometimes, she does take on the big sister role of the other two girls.

"*Gracias, cariño,*" I tell her honestly.

She nods and pulls her hair into a ponytail. "Let's get this house ready. I have a date tomorrow and I'd like to spend the evening preparing." She waggles her brows at us. "I have to shave everything."

All the girls giggle, including myself and Leticia.

My heart is full and I'm ready to face the day.

I'm just stepping out of Marco Antonio's room with my broom when I run into a giant, manly wall. Julio. He stops long enough to drop his gaze to my chest that is modestly secured behind my uniform. But it's as though he takes the time to imagine what's hiding in there. It causes a shiver to run up my spine.

He simply grunts as he staggers toward the stairwell at the end of the hallway. The sun is dipping below the horizon outside the windows and this creep is already drunk. I'm inclined to tell Arturo, but he's not here today. He and Alejandro have left to acquire some guns. I overheard that conversation when I was dusting the plants in the living room. Javier has been with Marco Antonio all day, showing the men entry points on the perimeter.

The men following him are straight-spined and serious. They'll do his bidding because Javier pays really well.

I'm shaken from my thoughts when I hear a door slam upstairs. Those girls better not be playing again. With my broom still in hand, I rush down the hallway and quietly up the stairs. All the doors are open. Yolanda is in one room with her headphones on dusting a ceiling fan. Silvia is scrubbing a bathroom down in another room. Her soft voice rings out as she sings. So that leaves Araceli. I walk down to the room that's to be Emiliano's. Earlier when I'd checked on them, she was unpacking toys for his stay.

I hear her cry out from beyond the door and anxiety floods through me. Julio headed up here moments before. So help me if he touches her…

I burst through the bedroom door and the scene before me stuns me for a moment. She's bent over the bed with her dress pushed up her hips and her panties wrenched down her thighs. Her legs kick and flail, but Julio is holding her down, working to get his cock out of his pants, is much stronger.

"¡Suéltala!" I yell, rushing forward. *Let her go!*

"*Vete, puta,*" he growls as he reaches for his weapon tucked in at his waistband behind him. *Leave, cunt.*

My instincts take over and I rush for him. I swing my broom hard against the side of his face. He lets out a groan of shock and then he's no longer interested in Araceli. Rage gleams in his eyes as he charges me. I strike him again, harder with the broom, and it breaks in half, hitting the wood floor with a clatter. He stumbles and knocks into the end table, sending the lamp crashing to the floor. His gun falls from his waistband and also hits the ground. Araceli redresses behind him and when our eyes meet, I see tears streaming down her cheeks.

He rushes for me again, but I drive the now pointed end of my broom into his gut and push him against the wall.

"You do not touch her," I hiss. "You do not touch any of them."

He reaches a long arm for me and grabs my throat. I can smell the tequila on his breath. I'm starting to see stars at his grip, so I push the pointed end of the broom harder into his stomach. Any harder and I'll break the skin. Obviously he doesn't care because he chokes me harder.

Pop!

His gun goes off and for a moment I worry I've been shot. But then I realize I'm staring at his lifeless eyes and blood is spattered all over the wall behind his head. I let out a surprised shriek the moment his hand falls from my neck and I rush backward, stumbling over my own feet. Araceli stands beside the bed with both arms raised, his gun in her grip. Her entire body trembles and tears don't stop rolling down her face.

"Araceli," I cry out. "What have you done?"

She turns her gun on me, a wildness in her eyes I've never seen. "H-He was going to r-rape me. I t-told him no." Her bottom lip quivers uncontrollably. "I was s-so scared."

"I know," I say, forcing my voice calm. "Hand me the gun, *cariño*."

Her arms drop and I rush over to take it from her grip. Marco Antonio bursts through the door, his eyes flaring with fury.

"What happened?" he roars.

Araceli flinches and I hug her into my arms. "He was assaulting her."

"He tried to rape me and I shot him," she explains, her voice shaking. "He was going to kill Rosa."

He glowers at us and I lift my chin. If I have to fight my way out of this room to protect us, I will. Marco Antonio may be big, but I do have a gun in my hand.

"Go to your rooms," he barks out. "I'll handle this."

As we pass, he yanks the gun from my grip. I allow it because I don't want to cause anymore strife. We've already done enough damage. I don't know what they'll do to us, but something tells me this won't go ignored.

Yolanda and Silvia are waiting in the hall with fear in their eyes. When they see us, they rush forward and envelop us in a sisterly hug that has my heart swelling. These people—the ones hugging me—are why I am here. To bring down bastards like Javier and his men in order to protect them. To protect other innocent people in this city who are prisoners in their own town because violent men run the streets destroying everything. Eventually it will happen. Every last one of them will be brought to justice in some way.

"Let's get to our rooms," I say, attempting to sound authoritative despite the shake in my voice. I quickly usher us through the house. Yolanda and Silvia retire to their room, but I bring Araceli into my room. She lies down on the bed and curls into a fetal position. Quickly, I fetch her some clothes from her room and then help her get comfortable. Once she's settled, I change out of my bloody dress and pace my room. I'll see Michael tomorrow and can report this to him, but protocol dictates that

I notify the agency immediately of anything detrimental like this.

You'll have to leave her alone.

I struggle with what to do. In the end, my job wins over. I kiss her temple and then change my clothes. After I ask the other two ladies to keep an eye on her, I leave the estate. It's getting dark and I hate to be out here so late by myself, but Michael and my superiors need to know of this latest development.

I stick to the shadows as I make it to the hotel. When I have emergency visits, I simply go to the front desk and ask how many rooms are available. Then I ask for which rooms are available with a view. And finally, which rooms have queen beds versus kings. Eventually, via process of elimination, I can figure out which room Michael will be in.

The walk over is uneventful, thankfully, and I learn that all the rooms but one are available. So I walk down the hallways and listen for sounds of movement. When I hear Michael's voice, I rap on the door ten straight times.

"Fuck." His muffled voice is filled with irritation. I try not to let it bother me. If I'm here the night before, there's a problem. That's what he's bothered about.

I swallow down the nerves that are eating me alive and stay strong. Tears threaten and I hate how weak I've become. I'd spent so many years hardening my heart from the outside world. But my girls and sweet Leticia back at the house have become family. I can't let anything happen to them. The lines of this job are becoming blurred. I'd never admit that to Michael or they'd have me pulled so fast my head would spin. By the end of next week, I'd be sitting at a desk in Virginia pushing paper around.

Screw that.

After what feels like way too long, the door opens wide. Michael's hair is messy and lipstick is smeared on his face. I blink in confusion. When a young woman with giant tits in a skintight yellow bandage dress walks past me, I let out a shocked sound. As soon as she exits through the door in the hallway, he ushers me inside and closes the door behind me.

"What is it?" he demands.

I scan the room. Takeout cartons litter the desk. The television plays some telenovela, but it's muted. A giant bottle of tequila sits beside the bed. The blankets are ruffled and I see three torn condom packages peeking out from under the bed. Bile rises in my throat and I turn my accusing glare to Michael.

"Are you...are you cheating on me?" His form blurs and distorts as tears stream down my cheeks.

He walks over to me and grabs my shoulders. The scent of tequila is strong on his breath. "We aren't anything, Rosa. You're my subordinate."

That's not what he said when he was fucking me every Saturday for four goddamned years.

"You asshole," I hiss and give him a shove.

He stumbles back and glowers at me. "Why are you here? What's going on?"

Angrily, I swipe at my tears with the back of my hand. "Araceli shot one of Javier's men to protect me. He's dead." A choked sob escapes me. "He was trying to rape her and I stepped in."

He charges forward and grabs my bicep. "Why did you step in? You know the rules, Daza. Stay the fuck out of their business. Just listen. Listen and report back. Your duty isn't to protect anyone." He gives me a hard shake and I yelp. "Were you made?"

I try to jerk from his grip, but his fingers bite harder into me. "N-No, I wasn't made. And I couldn't sit around and watch her get hurt!"

"Listen to yourself!" he roars. "You're losing your grip."

"I'm losing my grip?" I shriek. "You're fucking women behind my back. I thought you loved me! You've gotten so weird lately. You won't even have sex with me without your shirt on!"

It happens so fast.

His face becoming enraged. His hand rearing back. The exploding pain on the side of my head.

I crumple and fall to the floor, my palm tenderly caressing my cheekbone that smarts in pain. I'm dizzied and upset. My heart is crushed.

"Shit! Rosa," he grumbles, regret in his tone. "Goddammit. I didn't mean to do that. It's the fucking tequila. Come here, baby."

He sits on the floor and pulls me into his lap. A loud, ugly sob wracks through me and I clutch onto him despite him smelling like the woman who just left. Sweetly, he strokes my hair and kisses the top of my head.

"I'm sorry," he murmurs, hugging me tight. "I didn't mean it."

"I know," I say, although I don't really. But I do know I'm desperate for his affection.

"I'm under a lot of stress."

"Okay."

"I do love you," he murmurs. I stiffen because it's the

first time he's ever said it. "But…" I cringe as he continues. "But it's hard to have a relationship with someone you see for a few hours once a week."

My stomach hollows out. "I wish I could see you more."

"I know."

I sit up and look at him. Guilt shines in his gaze. He leans forward and kisses the corner of my mouth. I shouldn't want him, not still wearing that woman's lipstick and scent, but I do. I straddle his waist and cradle his face with my hands. We kiss slowly like teenagers and my heart sings.

"We can fix this," I breathe against his mouth. "I forgive you."

"I know we can," he assures me. "And as much as I'd love to do this all night and keep you with me, you need to tell me what happened. Then, you need to get back. I'll walk you there so you'll be safe. Tomorrow, on your day off, we'll talk more."

I hug him and nod.

We can fix this.

I think.

Capítulo Cuatro

Javier

Marco Antonio paces my office, his face bright red with rage. He looks like a fucking tomato. This man, my brother in most senses of the word, is losing his mind.

Over a maid.

With my brows lifted, I wait for him to explain again why I'm supposed care. Julio got his ass shot for trying to rape a maid. Big fucking deal. I thought that guy was sketchy to begin with. The only reason I kept him around was because he was strong and ruthless.

Not strong and ruthless enough, though, apparently, if a couple of maids could end him.

"Look at the footage. You'll see," he tries again.

I have enough bullshit to deal with. The last thing I care to do is play detective and watch a video of two scared maids fearing for their lives and killing in defense. I've seen enough of that in my lifetime. Hell, I've seen a little bit of everything. This is taking up precious time. What I want to discuss is the fact that Mayor Velez, a week later, hasn't given me what I asked for.

Money.

He owes me.

I've kept his name out of the media. I know all about his little addiction. And by little, I mean little. He has a thing for teenaged boys. If his wife knew, she'd cut his balls off. I know because I know everyfuckingthing there is to know about Guerrero. I paid him a visit last week and said he could pay me nine hundred thousand pesos to keep quiet, not that I needed the money anyway. He also promised he'd put the heat on Cielo, one of Acapulco's hottest night clubs, as long as I didn't show anyone the pictures I'd acquired of him and his little indiscretions. I promised because Club Cielo attracts a lot of tourists and I want it gone.

My end goal is to run every successful business out of Acapulco.

Send them straight to where my father has a giant portion of the market of hotels in Puerto Vallarta. It's a strategy we'd implemented years ago and have been working tirelessly on ever since.

I'm lost in my thoughts when Marco Antonio turns his laptop my way and points.

"Just watch," he orders.

I smirk, slightly amused at his bossy tone. As my second-in-command and my most trusted friend, he gets away with a lot of shit that not even Arturo or Alejandro would slide by on.

With eyes glued to the screen, I watch the young maid as she cleans. Julio enters the room. He must say something vulgar or frightening to her because she winces and backs away. She tries to get away, but he manages to pounce on her and pin her to the bed. He's just got her panties down her legs when *she* arrives.

I sit up because despite her hair being pulled back and not wearing any makeup, I know she's beautiful. I'd had the rare opportunity to see her up close last week rather than watching from afar as she cleans. My cock, which hasn't been interested in much lately, had thickened in my jeans. I'd wanted to fuck her right over the kitchen sink, but my brain reminded me I don't make rash decisions. I think them through. Fucking the maid— my best one no doubt—would have been an epic nightmare. She would've fallen in love or some shit. I'd have to let her go—or force her away depending on her level of clinginess—and then I'd have to deal with bringing another maid into my home to take her place.

Nobody else manages to adhere to my level of cleanliness like she does.

The other maids are good, but the head maid goes beyond what's expected of her. She may not think anyone notices, but I certainly do. I've noticed a lot about her in the years she's worked for me. And not just the way she cleans. I'm not immune to her full, luscious lips that were made for sucking cock. I can't ignore the way her juicy ass stretches the fabric of her maid's uniform. She's fucking hot, even though she tries her damnedest not to be.

My cock stirs and I ignore it as I watch the recording.

On the screen, she hits Julio with her broomstick. More fighting and then she breaks the broomstick on him. I snort when she stabs at his stomach with it. She's not afraid or trembling, no, she's fierce. Protecting the young one as though it's her duty. Julio struggles and then the young maid picks up the gun. The fucker is dead in the next instant. The head maid—*Rosa Delgado*—rushes over to the young one and plucks the gun from her grip. In the next moment, Marco Antonio shows up.

He pauses the video and then motions at the screen. "See?"

Leaning back in my chair, I shake my head. "I don't see. What I do see is a tough woman protecting one who was nearly raped. Moving on—"

"No," he growls. "I'm telling you. The way she hit him, with such force, and then the way she pinned him. That's professional, *jefe*."

I'm already bored of this conversation. I sit up and grab my pack of little cigars, desperate for a taste of candy apple nicotine. Plucking one from the pack, I light it and take a drag. The sweet smoke lingers on my tongue and instantly calms me.

I blow out a puff and sit back in my chair, thoughts of my mother lingering in my mind. Images of her when I was a young boy cutting apples for me and ruffling my hair. Pain lingers in my chest, but it's mostly dulled. My father ached for so long when we lost her. Sure, he's playing daddy to a new family now, but I don't know if he'll ever get over her death.

"What do you want me to do about it?" I demand. "Call her in here and spank her?" The thought is an enticing one. I'd seen the way her ass looked in her jeans. It's an ass worthy of a whipping, that's for sure. My cock hardens and I quickly push away thoughts of her ripe ass. The maid Marco Antonio is so worried about isn't a threat to me. If anything, I'm a threat to her.

"I just think we need to keep an eye on her." He runs his fingers through his hair. "And we need to deal with Araceli."

With my cigar between my teeth, I glower at him. "Who the fuck's Araceli?"

He rolls his eyes and it reminds me of when we were kids. Fucking dick. "She's the maid holding the smoking gun. Keep up here, asshole."

I take another drag of my sweet habit. "Call me an asshole again and I'll shove my fist up yours," I bark out, a plume of smoke clouding around me. "What do you plan on doing with her?"

"She's damaged goods now."

Sometimes Marco Antonio takes his job a little too damn seriously. "She's. A. Maid," I grit out. "This is a waste of my fucking time."

"You're right," he grunts. "I'll take care of it. Where are we on Velez?"

His sudden change of subject to more important matters has me sitting up and resting my little cigar in my ashtray.

"We're going to make the motherfucker wish he'd never been born," I growl.

He cracks his neck and grins at me. My brother of sorts and best friend has the ugliest mug I've ever seen, but he somehow lands a fuck-ton of women in his bed. I'll never understand that one. "Is he a dead man?"

"Right now, he's a man with a target on his back, but I want him in one piece. I want him taken to the shed."

His eyes darken with delight. Taken to the shed is a figure of speech. We have an empty manufacturing building, "the shed," in town that we use to torture, maim, and eventually kill. When motherfuckers mess up, we take them to the shed.

"I'll have Arturo and Alejandro round him up."

He leaves and I rise from my chair. I snuff out my cigar and walk through my house. It's quiet and one would almost assume it's empty, but it's filled with people who work for me. In another week, it'll be bustling with activity. I feel like I haven't seen Tania and Emiliano in ages. While Tania and I don't always see eye to eye, I have nothing but love for her son. My brother. I grin just thinking about the little shit. The kid is getting so big.

I'm walking through the house when I nearly get knocked over by a woman. It takes all of two seconds to gather my senses and realize it's *her*. Rosa Delgado. The feisty maid. Tonight, she doesn't look like she's been through physical hell like last week. More like literal hell. Her eyes are bloodshot, her button nose pink, and her fat lips swollen and red. A slight bluish bruise is forming on her cheekbone and I wonder if Julio gave that to her earlier.

"We have to stop running into each other like this," I tease as I steady her by her biceps.

All sadness bleeds from her expression and a flare of defiance flashes in her big brown eyes. My cock reacts—again—and I hold her right where I can look at her for a moment longer. Her hair isn't in a bun. Thick, wavy, cascading down her front like melted chocolate spilling down the side of a sundae. It makes me want to twist my fingers in it and see if she tastes like chocolate too.

"My apologies," she manages to croak out.

I look past her at the front door. "Where have you been?"

She stiffens. "Out."

Narrowing my eyes, I study her features. Deception flickers in her eyes and I wonder if Marco Antonio might

38

be onto something. She doesn't like my inspection because she forces her features calm and gives me a small fake smile.

"Do you need something, *señor*?"

You. On your knees. Putting those dick sucking lips to use.

"I always need *something, manzanita.*" *Little apple.*

She steps away from my hold and my hands fall to my sides. Her clothes are plain and not very feminine, but the curves she seems to want to try to hide scream for attention. They've certainly got *my* attention.

"How are the preparations coming for my father and his family?" I ask, stepping closer and enjoying the way she bumps against the pillar behind her. "You know, in between killing my men and all."

"I, uh..." she trails off and her eyes plead for me to understand.

I do understand. Women in this world are outmatched and hunted by the predators who go by the name *men*. She's lucky she has me for a boss. I am one of the few men in this country who knows you catch more flies with honey. The Estradas don't abuse women. Weak motherfuckers abuse women.

I am anything but weak.

"It's okay," I assure her. "Get some rest. There is still a lot to do. You know how picky my father is."

She nods quickly. Everyone knows my father is a spoiled sonofabitch. But he's the best man I know. He may love his food prepared a certain way and have his OCD tendencies, but he has always treated me as a business partner and his most prized possession. With Emiliano in the mix, he shares that love with his little boy, but I don't feel slighted in any way. He may be ruthless to others but first and foremost, my father is a family man.

"Rosa," I murmur as I run my knuckle along her cheekbone. "Put some ice on this."

She winces as though my words physically hurt her. It confuses me for a moment, but I step away to let her go. Perhaps she's got a lot more going on in that head of hers that she doesn't let others see.

But don't we all?

Capítulo Cinco

Rosa

She's gone.

I didn't notice until this morning, but Araceli is nowhere to be found. Her things remain in her drawers, but she's vanished. Yolanda, Silvia, and Leticia are all sick with worry, but nobody saw anything.

Jesus.

I knew I shouldn't have left last night.

They did something with her. Made her disappear or something. Oh, God, if they hurt her, I will cut every single one of their throats. I'm enraged as I check every closet and under each bed. I should be meeting with Michael since it's Saturday, but I refuse to do anything until I make sure she's okay.

I will find her.

When I walk past Javier's office, I pause. It's one of the few rooms without cameras. He keeps it locked when he's not in it. I'm one of the few people who has access since I have to get in there and clean. Maybe I could log in to the cameras and see who took her. Any kind of lead is a helpful one. I fish my keys out of my uniform dress pocket and push into his office. Quickly, I close and lock the door behind me. His laptop sits in the middle of his desk, so I rush over to it. I sit in his comfortable leather chair and snap open the computer. The office smells like him. Tobacco. Candy apples. Expensive, masculine scent. I don't admit to myself that I am kind of fond of the combination. Instead, I focus on finding Araceli.

His computer is password protected. I try several things before giving up. The key ring I've been given only has a few keys on it and his desk is not one of them. Yanking two bobby pins from my bun, I ignore the way my hair begins sliding from its neat position and I attempt to pick at the lock on the desk drawer. I'm still working at it when I hear keys jangling.

Oh, God.

He's coming.

I abandon the bobby pins in search of a hiding place. My quickest result is under the desk. I crawl underneath and try to make myself as small as possible. The door creaks open and footsteps across the wood floors can be heard as he approaches his desk. He whistles a jovial tune, something no cartel leader should even know how to sing, as he sits down in his chair. With him this close to me, in his lair, my heart rate thunders in my chest. Sweat breaks out over my flesh.

Maybe he won't see me.

He taps away on his computer.

Ping.

My eyes widen when I see the bobby pin that's fallen from the keyhole to the floor. I'm hoping he didn't hear it, but he slides away from the desk slightly. His muscled, tattooed arm reaches down to pluck it from the floor. I hold my breath and wait for him to continue working.

"I know you're down there, *manzanita*." His voice is low and threatening. "Question is, why?"

The breath I'd been holding onto escapes in a ragged rush. "I-I-I can explain."

I've barely gotten the words out before I'm being dragged out by my ankle. I let out a shriek of surprise. He fists the front of my uniform and hauls me to my feet.

Fuck. Fuck. Fuck.

I'm staring up at well over six feet of pure masculine glory. Javier is a lot of things. Ruthless. Cold. Murderous. Delinquent. But he's also fine. So damn fine. And his male parts right now are speaking to my female parts.

"Start talking fast," he murmurs, his brown eyes flickering with fury. Today, his black hair is slicked back and his cheeks are scruffy. The sides of his head have been recently shaven, accentuating the longer part on top. I'm not blind. He's hot. Ridiculously so. But it doesn't make him any less mean.

As if on cue, he pulls a knife from his pocket. A mewl escapes me when he gently pokes it into my side between two ribs. My mind whirs with an explanation, but I have none. I can't tell him I'm with the CIA. He'd do terrible things to me.

"Not fast enough," he hisses. He slides his knife to my middle button and he slices between the two folds of fabric. The button flips off and clinks to the floor. Panic rises up inside of me, but I'm frozen. He repeats his action for the bottom two buttons. I close my eyes when he slips his hand between the gaping material to touch me over my white cotton panties. "Cat got your tongue?"

I cry out in shock when he rubs his knuckle against

my clit. Our eyes clash together and evil dances in his gaze. Knowing he got a reaction, he repeats his action. I whimper, ignoring the jolt of pleasure, and push backward away from him. My ass hits the edge of the desk, locking me in.

"Talk to me, *manzanita*, or I'll cut every piece of clothing off you and *make* you talk. In fact, I'll make you scream," he threatens, his incessant rubbing on my clit dizzying me.

"I-I…w-was…just…"

He slides his hand into the top of my panties and his longest finger slips between the lips of my pussy. A groan pushes out of my mouth. Something resembling a feral growl rattles through him as his finger seeks my warmth. I'm so focused on what he's doing that I forget what I am…who I am…I forget everything. A thick finger pushes into me and I cry out. He curls it, his long digit stroking a place I never knew existed. I'm embarrassingly wet for him and I can't make sense of that.

I'm sick.

This shouldn't be happening.

I need to push him away and run.

His thumb finds my clit and he begins fingering me in a way that erases all my stress and worry. I'm with one of the biggest monsters the CIA is after and I'm willingly letting him bring me to orgasm.

"Tell me," he orders, his husky voice nearly my undoing. When I don't answer, he uses the knife to rid me of my top two buttons.

"I was looking for Araceli," I admit in defeat. I close my eyes and wait for him to slit my throat.

His fingers keep playing me until stars glitter behind

my lids. My knees buckle, but I don't fall. A harsh, unexpected orgasm ripples through me, drawing out a loud moan from me. I ride the waves until I feel dizzy. I'm blacking out. Either from pleasure or fear. He slips his finger from inside of me and pulls me against him. I can feel every single hard muscle in his chest through his T-shirt. My own chest is bare, aside from my bra. A bad man shouldn't feel this good. The tip of his blade scores the material along my spine. I bury my face against him in an effort to escape the knife.

"She is none of your concern," he demands lowly. "Your concern is this house. That is your job. That is what I pay you to do. Are we clear?"

I nod, hot tears leaking from my eyes and soaking his shirt. His hand cradles the back of my head and for a moment I wonder if he'll yank my head back and cut my throat. He doesn't cut me, though. Simply runs his fingers through my hair. The small act of affection, from a monster no less, has me sagging against him.

"I'm sorry," I breathe. "I was just worried about her."

"I've killed men for lesser offenses," he utters. "Don't get yourself killed because you're worried about a woman who is not even your blood."

He tosses his knife on the desk with a clatter. Then, his palm slides to my ass and his other hand keeps stroking through my hair. He squeezes my bottom and inhales my hair.

"It's your day off," he rumbles before stepping away. His intense brown eyes rake over the naked parts of my body, hunger flickering in his gaze. "Take the day off and come back to work tomorrow focused. Where will you go?"

I swallow. "To see my father."

"Good."

I clutch my dress together to hide my nakedness. My eyes drop to the floor. I can't look at him. His finger was inside of me. He just got me off. He is the enemy.

Fuck.

I push past him and all but run to the door. I'm just opening the door when his commanding voice stops me.

"Rosa, I will kill you if I have to."

His threat is loud and clear, reminding me he is evil and a monster.

I'm vulnerable.

In desperate need for comfort.

Ready to maul Michael.

After the confusing, terrifying, and hot moment with Javier, I've been on edge ever since. I'd gone back to my room and spent a lot of time getting ready. I borrowed one of Yolanda's yellow dresses and worked hard on my makeup. Winged eyeliner. Rosy cheeks. Dark, thick lashes. And blood red lips.

I barely recognized myself in the mirror.

Beautiful.

I knock on the door and Michael opens it. His gaze goes from bored to hungry in a matter of moments. I knew I could fix us. I'd grown too comfortable. Assumed he didn't need me to dress up for him. But he's a man, after all. He likes pretty things. And I'm a helluva lot prettier than that woman from last night, who I later learned was a prostitute.

Somehow knowing she was a whore and not someone who he actually had feelings for helped his betrayal
against me.

"Rosa," he murmurs.

I launch myself into his arms. Our lips meet and I
kiss him hard. His palms find my hips but instead of pulling me closer, he pushes me away.

"Stokes is waiting on a report. You're late," he reminds me. My red lipstick is smeared on his face and it
brings back memories from last night.

I drag myself away from him, ignoring the hurt
throbbing through me. "Something happened," I whisper. I'm playing a dangerous game, but my heart is calling the shots. I want him to feel the stab of hurt I felt.
"This morning, Javier caught me."

His eyes widen. "You were made?"

"What? No," I rush out. I'm about to tell him about
searching for Araceli, but then I remember the way he
struck me last night. He doesn't need to know the whys.
"I was in his office and I wasn't supposed to be. I'd ended
up hiding under his desk. He pulled me out and then…"

His brows scrunch together and his lips are pursed.
"Did he hurt you?"

"He fingered me," I whisper, my eyes wide.

He turns away from me and walks over to his computer. With his back to me, he says, "Did you like it?"

"What? Of course I didn't like it," I lie, my voice
shrill. I don't tell him I came harder than I ever have in
my life.

"So he knew you were snooping and then he fingered you before letting you go?"

"Yeah."

"This is perfect."

I blink in shock. "Excuse me?"

He turns and a devious grin is on his face. It crushes my heart that he doesn't even ask how I felt about it. "This is perfect. You can get closer to him. If he likes you, work that to your advantage. He'll give you access to information we desperately need." He motions at me. "Look at you, Rosa, you were made to seduce a man. You can do this."

"You're not mad?"

"I'm fucking thrilled," he elaborates. "This is the best progress we've had in years."

My heart sinks. "Stokes will think this is okay?"

"Stokes doesn't have to know right now. Just do more of this," he says as he motions to my dress.

He approaches me and I melt in his arms. Last night I didn't want to sleep with him because he'd had the prostitute here and my heart was broken, but today, I need to remind him why he wants me. I reach for my zipper and he swats my hand away.

"Leave it on, baby. It's too sexy to take off." He twists me and urges me to bend over the bed. With my palms on the covers, I try not to be bitter as he slides my dress up over my ass. He tugs my panties down and they drop to my ankles above my borrowed sandals. Within seconds his naked cock is out rubbing against my ass.

"Condom," I choke out, a shudder rippling through me.

"Right," he snaps. His tone is irritated.

I wait, my ass bared to him, for him to sheath his cock. He presses into me and I wince. I'm still aching from Javier's thick, expert finger. In a mechanical way,

Michael pistons against me.

Slapslapslapslapslap.

Our skins make sounds and it reminds me of earlier.

The sounds my body was making was wetter. Juicier. Needier. The barely stifled moans coming from me were desperate and wild. A jolt of pleasure trickles through me at the reminder. I want Michael to get me off, to bring me back into the moment with him, but he's focused on his own release.

What am I even doing?

One sick, twisted morning in Javier Estrada's office and I'm suddenly questioning everything with Michael.

The thought is a dangerous one.

Have I been undercover too long? Am I losing my mind?

Michael comes with a hiss and I feel his heat rushing out, thankfully protected by the condom. I'd always wanted to protect myself against pregnancy since I'm in no point in my life ready to be a mother, but after last night and seeing that prostitute, I want to protect myself from much more. He pulls out and deposits the condom in the restroom. I jerk my panties up my thighs and cross my arms, my stance defensive.

"Let's have dinner together," I murmur.

He rights his clothes and scowls. "I've got work to do." He points at the door. "And so do you."

I glower at him, a spark of the real me climbing to the surface. I've spent four years being someone else that I've nearly snuffed out Rosa Daza. I flip him off and start for the door. I've just yanked it open when he grips my elbow painfully.

"Rosa," he snaps. "What the fuck is your problem?"

I try to jerk my arm from his grip to no avail. "I'm just so over this," I admit, tears threatening.

"There is no *this*," he reminds me. "There was never a *this*."

I recoil at his harsh words. "Let me go."

"I'll walk you home," he offers as he releases me. "It's dark."

"No need," a deep, dangerous voice rumbles from the hallway. "I'll take over from here."

Javier Estrada, dressed to the nines in a fancy pale gray three-piece suit, is leaned against the scummy peeling wallpaper looking incredibly out of place. I'm frozen to the dirty carpet, a deer caught in the headlights.

How much did he hear?

He must read my expression because he chuckles. "He doesn't look old enough to be your father. But it appears I misunderstood. He's your *daddy*." He smirks as he straightens and steps forward.

Michael pushes past me, his body blocking mine from Javier's approach. My heart sails at his protecting me. "We're nothing anymore. We broke up."

Pain cuts through my abdomen.

I think the words are more for me than Javier.

Javier's brown eyes dart to mine and he gauges my reaction. I flinch because, in essence, that's exactly what just happened. Bowing my head, I attempt to calm my nerves.

"Come, *manzanita*," Javier says, his voice commanding and somehow soothing all at once. "I will escort you." He opens his jacket to reveal his piece strapped to his body. Not only is he always carrying, but he's like the big man in this city. The one they all fear, worship, or respect. With him, nobody would touch me.

"We can still be friends," Michael murmurs. "I'll take you out to dinner on your next day off." His eyes pin me and I know he wants me to play along.

I give him a clipped nod that I understand. I understand the mission, but I do not understand why he's thrown my heart in the blender. Has it always been one-sided? Michael retreats into the room and closes the door. I'm left standing alone with my boss, leader of the cartel, and the man whose finger was inside of me this morning. I'm caught somewhere in between my chest aching from Michael being so cold to my skin feeling inflamed from Javier's scorching stare.

"Have you eaten?" he asks, his voice low so that if Michael is listening, he can't be heard.

I lift my eyes and regard him in confusion. "Why are you here? Did you follow me?"

His gaze rakes over my dress and he flashes me an impish grin. "I followed the dress, *mami*." His dimple forms and a flash of heat surges through me.

Seduce him.

Simple.

I can do this.

Capítulo Seis

Javier

"The dress wasn't for you," she throws back at me saucily.

Oh, the dress *was* for me. The moment I caught a glimpse of her walking by in that dress, I knew it was for me. I'd stood and followed her right out of the house, knowing that every asshole in Acapulco would want a piece of my hot fucking maid in her little yellow dress. And I needed every single one of them to know it was *my* dress. *My* maid. *Mine.*

"Of course not, *manzanita.*" I smirk at her as I offer her my elbow.

She eyes it warily, her normally completely composed demeanor shattered from that fuckwad. Her *father.* The stink of sex permeating from the room when the door opened had my hackles raised. I may not have truly spoken to her much during her employment, but I'm not blind. A man can identify a gorgeous woman when she lives in his home and cleans his space. Her scent—sweet like apples—clings to my belongings, and quite frankly, I enjoy it.

But if there's anything my *padre* ever taught me, it's

52

don't fuck the people you pay to do you a job. Feelings cloud their judgment and then you lose someone good because you couldn't keep your dick in your pants.

For four years, I've appreciated her feminine curves and attention to detail. Yet, the night when she showed up battered in the kitchen, she awoke something inside me. Curiosity if you will. A desire to bend my father's rules. Bend her. Specifically, over my desk.

She lets out a heavy sigh and clutches onto my elbow. "You don't have to take me home. I can walk."

Over my dead body.

Last time, she almost got herself killed.

"I'm not taking you home," I rumble as we walk through the scuzzy hotel. When I'd followed her, I called Alejandro and asked him to meet me at the hotel. And as we walk outside, he's standing beside his white Hummer with his arms crossed against his chest. His eyes widen slightly as he takes in the sight of Rosa.

Appreciation.

I think she has the same effect on every man who crosses her path.

Well, except the overweight, balding motherfucker who clearly fucked her one last time before breaking her heart. *That* I will never comprehend.

Leaning into her as we walk, my lips brush against her hair. "He is blind and fucking stupid."

She stiffens but gives me the briefest nod. I smirk as I guide her to the passenger side of the vehicle. Her brows scrunch together when I open the door for her.

"You don't have to be so nice," she mumbles as she slides in. Her short yellow dress rides up her tanned thighs as she settles on the leather seat.

I grab the seatbelt and reach across her chest, my arm brushing against her fat tits as I buckle her in. "Who says I'm nice?" I arch a brow at her. Our faces are inches apart—so close I can almost taste her. The idea of having her is becoming every bit a goal of mine as all the shit I do for my father.

It's what we Estrada men do.

We calculate, we conquer, we own.

Right now, I'm calculating how I can make this happen without having it blow up in my face. I'll read her tells and pay attention to her personality. Once I've deduced she isn't going to go batshit crazy after a wild fuck or two, then I will conquer her sweet, supple body. And I already fucking own her, so that's that.

She clears her throat and Alejandro chuckles under his breath from the backseat. I ignore him and close her inside. Once I'm in the driver's seat, I scan the streets. This evening is semi calm. Normally, I'd be stirring shit up to keep the momentum of this city's descent into hell going. But not now. Now, I need to take care of fucking business.

When we pass the estate, Rosa sits up and jerks her head my way, suddenly alert and not feeling sorry for herself. "Where are we going?"

"Errands."

Another snort from the backseat.

"Are we going to go get Araceli? Is she safe?" She turns in her seat and bites on her bottom lip. It's plump and painted red. Fuck, she's hot. And she isn't even trying. The woman doesn't even realize she's so goddamned pretty.

"She's fine—" Alejandro offers from the backseat,

but his words die in his throat when he catches my furious glare in the mirror.

At hearing this, she relaxes some, but I don't miss the way her eyes scan the roads. She's vigilant. Always watching. It's something I've noticed about her at the house. Nothing gets by her with her staff. Makes me wonder how much of *my* shit she notices.

Marco Antonio's words buzz in my head.

"I'm telling you. The way she hit him, with such force, and then the way she pinned him. That's professional, jefe."

I flit my gaze over to her hands. She wrings the bottom of her dress in a nervous manner. If she was fucking spying like Mr. Conspiracy Theory thinks, she'd be relaxed. Not this. The woman is rattled. A bit curious but mostly uneasy. But she's riding around with Guerrero's biggest monster. A devil in an expensive suit with a disarming smile. She better feel unnerved.

She doesn't ask any more questions until we pull up to the shed.

"Stay," I bark, pinning her with a hard stare. "I'll be back in fifteen minutes."

Alejandro grumbles. "I don't get to come, do I?"

He knows his job. Fucking babysit my hot maid.

"Nope."

"Figures. I really hate that dickhead."

I shrug as I climb out of the Hummer. "I'll save you a finger."

Rosa gasps, but I don't spare her a glance. Most women in the city know the level of crime here. And, she of all people, knows I'm the one who stirs the fucking pot. I stride over to the key panel and punch in the code. I'm gained entry and I step into the dark metal building.

As soon as the door slams closed behind me, I hear him.

"Help! Someone help me!"

Velez.

I crack my neck and roll it along my shoulders to stretch out the tension. Having Rosa on my mind is screwing with my thoughts. It's not often I'd prefer to take home a woman than rip off a man's fingers with a pair of pliers.

I walk through the empty building until I find the room in the back. Bright light shines below the door. Pushing into the room, I let satisfaction roll through me to see my victim sitting bound to a chair.

Naked.

Mayor Velez *likes* to get naked after all.

With fucking underage boys.

As soon as he sees me, his face crumples. Tears stream down his face and I haven't even done anything. Yet.

"*Buenas tardes, Alcalde.*" *Good evening, Mayor.* I unbutton my smoke-gray linen Versace jacket and slide it down my arms. I hang it from a hook on the wall. This suit cost me nearly fifty-six thousand pesos. I'm not keen on soiling it with the mayor's blood, sweat, and tears. A lightweight durable suit where you don't sweat your balls off in the Acapulco heat is hard to come by.

"N-No, p-please," he begs.

Ignoring him, I walk over to the far wall and pull down my rubber apron. I slide it over my head and tie it around my back. The putrid scent of piss fills the air and I groan. Thank fuck the little shit is sitting over a drain. When I'm done with him—whenever that might be—I'll hose him down and all evidence of our fun will slide down the tiny hole at his feet.

"I can get you the money."

"You didn't, though," I say as I unbutton my cuffs and start rolling one sleeve up.

"I needed m-more t-time, *Señor* Estrada." He sobs. *"P-Por favor."*

He begs and pleads as if this will sway my decision. I roll up my other sleeve to my elbow and then walk over to the toolbox. "You know how things work, *hijo de puta*." I hold up a hammer and inspect it in the light before setting it down. "You obey or you don't." I pick up the pliers. *"Sencillo."* Simple.

"Not simple," he argues, his voice reaching shrill heights. "M-My wife. She would have killed me for t-taking the money from our savings and—"

"I. Will. Kill. You," I roar as I stalk over to him. My Gucci leather shoe splashes in his piss puddle and it makes me want to grab him by his thinning hair so I can punch his fucking skull in. Dealing with this motherfucker was not on the agenda. Hours ago, I had my finger inside the tight pussy of a beautiful woman. Had this asshole not fucked up my day, who knows where I would've gotten with her. But now I have to go get back into the car with her smelling like this dickhead's piss.

"I promised my bodyguard I'd bring him a souvenir," I say with a manic grin. "I wonder what he'd like. A finger? A toe? Your tongue?"

He trembles, but there's nowhere for him to go. His wrists are bound behind him and tied to the chair. Each ankle is tied to a leg of the chair. I lift my leg and step on his small, limp old man cock with my soiled shoe, pressing it into the chair beneath him. He howls in pain when

I dig my toe forward, smashing his balls too.

"Please d-don't cut off my penis," he begs, snot running from his nose over his salt and pepper mustache.

"Oh, Velez, such little imagination. You've been watching too many American eighties movies. I'm not the bad guy from a Sylvester Stallone movie. Nobody is coming to save you. You're not going to free yourself from your bindings and punch your way out of this shit." I playfully slap his sweaty face. "And I'm not going to cut your little pecker off. I don't have my tweezers with me to find the damn thing," I say, my lips turning up in a predatory smile. "The things I have planned for you are *much* more violent."

"N-No, please! I have money in my safe at my office. The code is 87654. Take it all. Just take it all."

I let up on smashing his cock and balls and step away from him. Reaching into my pocket, I pull out my phone. I hold up a picture of his wife. "I talked to Val."

"Don't hurt her. She's innocent," he chokes out.

I laugh so hard tears spring to my eyes. "You fool. You fucking fool. Your sweet wife is not innocent. You should have heard the swear words coming out of her mouth when I told her about your little addiction. At first she didn't believe me, but I showed her the pictures. The latest kid. He's what, same age as your son?" I shake my head at him. "Your wife gave me the money."

"W-What? She paid you to protect me from my shame?"

Another dark laugh. "No, Velez. She paid me to make you fucking suffer."

His eyes grow wide with horror. "She wouldn't."

I flip to the video recording of Val. She's destroying

his home office and screaming. Tears stream down her face. When I told her how many boys and the extent of her husband's perversions, she cracked. Went fucking mad. In the recording, she turns her tearstained, hate-filled face to the camera. "I hope you suffer," she hisses. "I hope you suffer slowly."

I end the recording and pocket my phone. Velez sobs. Val is packing her shit as we speak and moving out of the city. Nobody, not even in a crime-ridden city, wants to be associated with that sort of horror. Even fucking criminals have to draw the line somewhere. That makes Velez the lowest of the low.

With my back to Velez, I whistle to a new Luis Fonsi song I heard at the club last week as I choose a long, thin wire from my toolbox. Once I'm satisfied with one that'll do the job, I turn and face the piece of shit. He's purple and practically hyperventilating. I keep whistling and dance my way back over to him, careful not to splash in his piss. Squatting in front of him, I push his laughable, urine dripping cock out of the way and grab hold of his big-ass balls. He squeals like a goddamned stuck pig when I pull his nuts toward me.

"You might feel a little pinch," I taunt, baring my teeth at him. When will the men in this city learn you don't fucking blow off an Estrada? They should have learned from my father. They sure as hell should have learned from me. Word gets around. These motherfuckers know who runs this show.

I wrap the thin wire around his balls and twist it. Then, I latch the pliers onto the twisted wires and begin turning. His screams get louder and louder as I twist the metal. Each turn makes his balls bulge more and turn purple. Once I'm close to breaking the skin but still tight enough to hurt like a motherfucker, I stop. I rise to my feet and ruffle his drenched-from-sweat hair.

"Someone will be by each day to give it a few turns." I grin at him as I step away and walk over to the wall. "Eventually those fuckers are going to fall right off." I toss the pliers into the box and yank off the hot-ass apron. "I told you I wasn't the type of man to cut your dick off." I shrug as I hang my apron. "Now Marco Antonio? I can't promise he won't be feeding you your own cock later for dinner."

He screams and cries as I wash up at the sink. Once I've got that sick fuck's ball sweat off my hands, I grab my jacket and toss it over my shoulder. Another song flips into my mind and I start whistling that one as I leave Velez to sit and stew about what happens when you fuck with Javier Motherfucking Estrada.

You lose.

Capítulo Siete

Rosa

I step out of my shower, newly cleaned but still harboring a lot of pain. After Javier showed up out of the blue this evening, I'd been reeling. I kept waiting for him to reveal he knows who I am. *What* I am. But he didn't. Simply took me to the shed.

The shed.

One of the locations that have alluded the CIA for years. He simply drove straight to it with me in tow.

I'm not a threat.

Even after him catching me snooping, he didn't feel as though he needed to keep such a private thing from me. By digging around a little deeper, he let me in.

Michael is right.

I do need to do this.

Seduce the one-dimpled, sexy-as-sin monster.

My core throbs at the reminder of him touching me. If I'm to seduce him, the prospect of him touching me more is a very real idea.

Images of myself naked and beneath that beast of a man flip through my mind fast enough to catch fire. A mewl escapes me. That would be terrifying. Right?

I'm having a hard time convincing myself.

If I'm going to have to fuck Javier Estrada, willingly, then I'm going to need a drink. I walk out of my bathroom once I'm dried and hunt down something sexy. Of course, I own nothing. In the end, I choose a tank top and a short pair of cotton shorts. My pajamas. I groan but don't give up. I leave my wet hair down to air dry and quickly put on some makeup. Just enough to look like I didn't put any on. I do, though, make sure to apply a dark shade of red on my lips. Every man loves red lips, I'd assume.

Once I'm satisfied that I look decent enough, I slide on some flip-flops and sneak past the girls' room. When I'd come home earlier, Yolanda and Silvia were still out. Leticia made me some dinner and pouted when I picked at it. Nobody, including me, knows where Araceli is, but at least Alejandro slipped and indicated she was fine. It gives me hope.

I make my way downstairs and rummage around in the liquor cabinet in the kitchen. There is liquor all over this house, but the kitchen has what I want. Tequila. I grab the bottle and head to the back patio. I'll get some liquid courage in my veins and then I'll seek out Estrada. I know he's here.

The wind is cool and hard enough that it hisses through the trees. I unscrew the bottle and take a long pull on the alcohol. It burns as it slides down my throat. Since I'm always on the job, I don't drink. I forgot how gross it is. Groaning, I tip the bottle again. I swallow down some more, but my esophagus is already on fire, so it isn't as difficult to drink this time.

I plop down on a lounger and watch leaves blow into

the pool. I make a mental note to have Pablo scoop them out tomorrow. With Yoet coming, I know Javier will want the heated pool ready. His father enjoys swimming.

Sometimes, I look out past the beautiful home and watch the waves. For just a few moments, I can pretend I'm on vacation. Lord knows I need one. I imagine I'm at a fancy hotel and allow myself to dream. Much like I did when I was a young girl. Before all hell broke loose and destroyed my life. Back then, I imagined growing up to be beautiful like my mother. I wanted to marry someone who was just as handsome and fearsome as my father. I realize now that was ridiculous, but at the time it was a girly dream.

In the end, I chose retribution.

I chose a career.

Family and marriage and white picket fences are for soft people. I'm too hard for all that. I started hardening the day I watched my mother bleed out on a greasy kitchen floor.

Tears flood, thanks to the alcohol, and I don't hold them in. I drink the warming tequila and welcome the fall. My heart that wasn't very big to begin with suffered its final blow tonight. I'd been reaching and hoping for something with Michael. A small step toward a sliver of happiness. An almost happily ever after. It felt attainable.

But for my every tug for this relationship, he pulled away.

My bitter heart aches for the loss of him.

A part of me is furious at him. I'm a strong, educated, brave woman—imbedded in the hornet's nest. Each day I stare at the face of danger on behalf of the CIA. I'm a catch. Right?

What does Michael, besides being my superior, have over me that makes him better than me? What makes him think it's okay to fuck me and then fuck whores behind my back?

Rage bubbles up inside me. Hot and violent. I won't take him back. Ever. Over the past four years, we've had our ups and downs, but for some stupid reason, I forgave him. I give and give and give.

He takes and takes and takes.

Fuck, Michael.

A low, deep voice rumbles behind me. "Yeah, fuck, Michael."

I nearly drop the bottle of tequila. "You scared the crap out of me."

Javier emerges from the shadows on the side of the house with his hands in his pockets. His big, expensive watch catches the moonlight and flashes. He's changed from earlier, his hair wet from a recent shower. My gaze roves over his white T-shirt that molds to his impressive chest. His black track pants hug his muscled thighs and my mouth waters.

I can do this.

It's not like he's a dog.

He's a fine-looking man.

Seducing him will be second nature.

"Storm's coming," he murmurs as he walks past me. He rests his forearms on the railing and I get a nice view of his ass.

"Yep," I agree as I swallow more tequila.

He turns and flashes me a dimpled grin that makes my thighs clinch. "Better slow down on that tequila, *manzanita*, or you'll end up naked in my bed."

I laugh at his arrogance. "You wish, baddie."

He walks over to me and pries the tequila bottle from my grip, his fingers brushing against the back of my hand, sending hot currents of excitement coursing through me. "Baddie?"

With the liquor burning through my veins, I feel bolder. I poke his hard stomach. "Yep. *El Malo*," I mock, making my voice deep like a man. "The bad. And you're the king baddie."

His dimple reappears as he brings the bottle to his lips. I lick my own because damn he's making me thirsty. He tilts his head back and swallows, his Adam's apple moving as he drinks.

"Well, if you work for the king baddie," he says with a black eyebrow raised, "what does that make you, *criada*?"

I shrug as I grab the bottle and take another drink. "The bad maid?"

He chuckles as he reaches down and curls his strong hand around my wrist. I'm tugged to my feet easily. Dizzy on my feet, I sway slightly. His hands find my waist to steady me. "You're a good maid, *mami*. So good." His dark eyes flicker with hunger.

I want to get eaten.

A giggle bursts from me. "You want to eat me."

His lips turn up in a wolfish grin. "I sure do. I bet you taste like sweet, succulent apples."

"I—" A scream rips from me the moment I see one of the lawn chair cushions blowing away. The bottle falls from my grip and hits the deck, shattering.

A strong arm wraps around my waist and he lifts me while simultaneously pulling a gun from his waistband.

He swings it around to shoot at whatever I screamed at. His quick movements to protect me have my heart swelling in my chest.

"It's gone," I complain, my bottom lip pouting out. My feet dangle as he holds me in his grip.

His nose nuzzles my hair and he inhales me, sending blasts of need rippling through me. "What's gone, Rosa?"

"The cushion."

He chuckles against my hair as he tucks his gun behind him back into his pants. "You scared the fuck out of me, *mami*."

My flesh heats. "Don't tell anyone a little ol' maid can scare the big bad baddie of them all."

He walks us away from the mess and drops me to my feet. His arm stays curled around me, just under my breasts. "You shouldn't scream like that unless you're getting hurt or when my mouth is latched onto your cunt."

I tremble in his grip. Fear is the last thing I'm feeling right now. My plan to seduce him is almost too easy. A job perk if you will. I want him to slide his palm under my shirt and pinch my nipple. "Nobody cares about them."

"Who?"

"The lawn chair cushions."

His lips press against my hair and he turns his body to press his cock against my backside. I'm locked in his grip and I'm not looking to escape.

"You're right," he says, amusement in his tone. "Nobody fucking cares about the lawn chair cushions."

"I do," I say with a huff, genuinely offended.

"Because you're the good maid," he growls, his thumb sliding over my erect nipple through my tank top.

"The best maid. My favorite one, in fact."

I melt against him and tilt my head to the side. I like him touching me. I like him whispering things to me and touching me so sweetly. I've been so starved of affection that I'm desperate for what he offers.

"What's wrong with me?" I ask suddenly, tears prickling my eyes again.

His lips seek my neck, giving me what I silently ask for. "Nothing, *manzanita*. Absolutely nothing." He runs his tongue along my flesh, causing me to shiver. "You let *Michael* fill your head with filth. He's a loser and undeserving of such a gem." His teeth nip at my skin. "Could he even make my good little maid come?"

I roll my head back against him. With the tequila turning my bones to molten lava, I melt at his words and touch. I'm greedy to prolong whatever it is that's happening. In fact, I want to encourage it.

"He did in the past," I admit. "Not recently."

"Tonight?"

I stiffen and my heart aches as tears well in my eyes. "I felt used."

His thumb brushes along my nipple again. "He fucked you?"

Bitter tears roll down my cheeks and I sniffle. He presses sweet kisses along my neck to my ear. His large palm cups my breast and his other one slides from my hip to between my thighs. He grips me possessively over my shorts in a claiming sort of way.

"He fucked me," I whisper, my voice shaking. "I wanted him to even though I caught him with a prostitute." A sob catches in my throat. "I used to not be like this. So weak."

His longest finger rubs my clit over my shorts. Slowly but expertly. "You are not weak," he whispers. "You are fierce."

I am fierce.

Fierce, strong, smart.

I needed the reminder.

"I'm going to make you come," he utters, his voice sure and unwavering. He continues his unhurried assault, successfully making my panties grow wet for him. An embarrassing moan climbs from my throat. "That's it, Rosa, let me show you how it feels to be with a real man."

Stars glitter around me as my orgasm nears.

God, I want more.

"Javier," I whisper.

"Sweet woman," he rumbles. "My name on your lips is torture."

"I need..."

I don't know what I need. I don't know why I'm here. I don't even know who I am anymore. But this... this I need. This man touching me and making my body come alive. This man whispering things that awaken the battered soul that has been haunting this body.

His finger leaves my pussy, causing me to whine, but then his giant hand is delving into my shorts past my panties. I cry out when his hot fingers seek out my soaked flesh. He pushes a finger past my opening, wetting it, before he slides it back up to my clit. It's slippery and it gives him the movement he's searching for. With quick, expert circles, he brings me to orgasm. His name bursts from my lips and my knees buckle.

I'm spent.

Dizzy and confused and spent.

And now I'm flying.

I'm in Javier's arms and he's striding through his massive estate. He carries me to his bedroom. The moment his masculine scent that is strongest in his room hits my nose, a sliver of panic flitters through me.

He tosses me on the bed and his eyes flare with hunger. Suddenly shy, I cross my legs.

"You can't hide from me now," he says with a grin, his dimple making an appearance. "You're in my lair now and I'm starved."

I wait for him to pounce and take me, but instead he lowers the lights and places his phone on a music dock. He scrolls through some songs and then lands on a fairly new Mexican band I've heard on the radio a few times. The singer's voice is sultry and almost pleading as he croons for his love to understand who he is behind the many faces he's forced to wear.

My eyes clash with Javier's. His hair is messy and it makes him appear younger than his thirties. He reaches behind him to grab hold of his T-shirt and he pulls it off his body. When he tosses it at me, I let out a surprised laugh.

"Hey," I grumble.

"I had to do something to distract you," he teases. "Your eyes were going to roll right out of your head."

But he was wrong...

Now my eyes are going to pop out. His chiseled chest is on full display, making my mouth water. Tattoos litter his flesh, but the most eye-catching one is El Malo scrawled across his lower abdomen right between the hard edges of his "V" written in a script font. The "o" on the word doesn't end but curls a black line that whips around and dips below the waistband of his pants. I'm still gaping at his perfect body when something flashes, catching my attention.

His gun.

He's pulled it from his back and it hangs at his side in his grip. For a second, I worry he knows and he's going to shoot me. Yet, he doesn't. He simply sets it on the end table. Another song comes on and his hips start moving. I become mesmerized in the way he dances.

It's hypnotic.

Relaxing.

Safe.

I close my eyes and let the tension bleed from me as I listen to the song. He starts singing along and I'll be damned if I don't find myself singing along too.

Capítulo Ocho

Javier

I know the moment she wakes because her soft, languid body becomes rigid at my side. Rain pelts the windows outside this morning and the storm keeps my bedroom dark. I'm not keen on getting out of this bed.

Not when I have this sexy and very naked woman wrapped around me.

Her palm is on my chest, her full tits pressed to my side, and she slowly fists her hand. I guess tequila is making her regret last night. Does she even remember last night?

"Buenos dias, hermosa," I greet, my voice raspy from sleep.

She peels herself off me and sits up. Her dark hair is messy and out of control. Cute, swollen lips part as she takes in our nakedness. "Oh, God."

I smirk at her and run my knuckle over her nipple. "Yes, ye faithful servant?"

Her lips twitch for a moment like she might smile, but then she's pulling away from me, dragging the sheet with her. My cock gets exposed to her and I lazily grab hold of my morning wood.

"*Señor* Estrada," she hisses, her wide eyes watching my movements. "Did we…"

"Fuck?"

She winces and nods.

"Not yet, *mami*. Not yet."

"I, uh, I need to get to work," she starts, her gaze never leaving my moving hand.

"Today's your day off."

"Yesterday was my—"

"Today's your day off," I growl.

She starts to slide off the bed, but before she can get all the way away from me, I grab the sheet and yank it to me. A squeal escapes her as she goes with the sheet, desperate to hide every sweet curve from me as though I didn't spend hours staring at her while she slept last night.

"If we didn't have sex, why am I naked?" she asks, jerking at the sheet.

"You stripped off all your clothes when 'Despacito' came on." Fuck, was that shit hot. "And then you passed the hell out." That made my erection practically weep.

"And you, uh, didn't force me?" Her brows furl together as she regards me warily.

"No, I didn't force you," I snap as I abandon my cock to fist the sheet. I yank it off of her and toss it away. Then, I pounce on her.

She screams and takes a swing at me, but I easily overpower her as my body slides on top of hers. I grab her wrists and pin her to the bed. Her tits jiggle as she breathes heavily, fear of me rippling from her in waves. My cock is hard pressed against her thigh.

"Javier," she whimpers.

Fuck, I love my name on her lips.

I'd love to put my cock there too.

"Sí."

"I…" Tears well in her eyes. Shame. Fear. Confusion. Now that I've homed in on her, I see *everything* about her. "I don't want this." She closes her eyes and a tear leaks out, running down her temple.

I bind her wrists with one hand. Her body stiffens and her bottom lip trembles. With my free hand, I stroke my fingers through her unruly chocolate locks, working out the tangles. When she realizes I'm not about to force myself on her, her brows scrunch and she flutters her eyes open.

"You have a lot of pain in your heart," I murmur, my thumb running along her jaw.

Her nose turns pink and her nostrils flare. "What heart?"

Our eyes meet, hers blazing as though she dares me to challenge her. I slide my palm down her throat and rest it between her perfect bouncy tits.

"This one." The beat of her heart pounds against my hand. Hard. Fast. Very much alive and present.

She turns away to stare out the window. The storm is unrelenting. Wind howls outside, rattling the entire house.

"It's in the past," she whispers. Her pain, so palpable I can almost taste it, reminds me of *my* past.

And when I suffered pain all those years ago, I needed a distraction.

Rosa needs a distraction.

Leaning forward, I suck her nipple into my mouth.

She gasps and her back arches up off the bed, feeding me more of her sweet tit. I groan against her flesh before biting the hardened peak and pulling it. My eyes flit up to hers. She's staring at me, her lips parted, with the hottest fucking expression on her face. I release her nipple from my teeth and circle the tender skin with the tip of my tongue. Her breathing is heavy and her stare is intense. With one simple look, she dares me. She urges me on as though I don't have plans to devour her entire body.

Sweet Rosa, I plan on tasting every inch of you.

I release her hands and start kissing down her stomach. She lets out a mewled sound, her breathing becoming more intense.

"I'm going to release you because I need two hands for what I'm about to do to you," I growl and nip at her soft flesh near her belly button.

"I don't…" she trails off when I let go of her hands to continue kissing down her stomach.

"Spread your legs and let me see how wet you are," I demand, darting my eyes to her as I tease her skin just above her pubic bone. Her cunt is smooth shaven and I approve of how perfect it is.

"You haven't even kissed me yet," she says in a breathless tone.

I blow a soft breath on her pussy. "Let me rectify that, *mami*." I press my lips to her clit. Her body jolts, spurring me on. I grip her knees and pry her apart for me. Her lips open up to me as if they're inviting me in. My tongue flits out and I lick her from her opening to her clit where I circle it in a teasing way with my tip.

"There," I breathe against her soaked cunt. "Our first kiss."

Her fingers seek out my hair and she clenches it in her fists. "Kiss me some more." The needy way in which she begs has my cock dripping with pre-cum. I want inside her so bad it physically hurts. But I'm very much enjoying taking my time with her too.

Rosa Delgado is in my mind.

Settling herself in there and getting fucking comfortable.

It's a place I don't let anyone in, and I'm not sure if I even like it.

But what I do like is the way her body comes alive at my touch. How my serious, always so composed maid loses her fucking mind with my tongue between her legs.

"Javi," she says sharply, her fingers tugging at my hair.

I growl against her pussy and flatten my tongue against her. Licking and licking like one would a big lollipop, I taste the sweetness that gushes from her body. My fingers dig into her thighs and I push them up. I like the way her hole peeks open as if showing me a secret entrance only meant for me. Pushing my tongue into her tight hole, I revel in the way she screams—fucking screams—at the intrusion. I could eat this pussy for days, enjoying all her reactions. Certainly does a fuck-ton for my ego knowing she's absolutely hypnotized by me.

I fuck her hole with my tongue as my thumb slides to her clit. She's soaked and dripping. The slurping sounds are erotic and I fucking love them. Her arousal and my saliva run down the crack of her ass. It makes me want to be there too. As I rub her clit and fuck her cunt, I slip my other hand to her asshole. She cries out when I push against the puckered entrance. It's slick and lubricated, just begging to be taken there as well. I inch my finger in slowly.

"Oh!"

I grin and increase my attention on as many places as I can touch, taste, and feel. The moans coming from her are the hottest thing I've ever heard. And just when I think she can't take any more, she shatters.

Completely comes undone.

Her ass clenches around my finger at the same time her cunt spasms around my tongue. I don't stop the circling of my thumb on her clit as she comes. She jolts and shudders. When I think she may be coming down from her high, I work her harder and faster. A shriek of surprise belts from her.

"Too much!" she cries out. "Javi!"

I groan against her. I love the way the shortened version of my name sounds as she moans it. So addictive, this woman. She comes again, harsher and wilder. The pull on my hair has me growling in warning because it fucking hurts. But this sweet, exploding woman doesn't care she's about to scalp a cartel king.

All she cares about is coming.

When she falls limp, I ease my finger and tongue out of her. I crawl up her body, my dripping cock desperate for some pleasure too. My erection rubs against her. Her eyes are heavy-lidded and her lips are parted. With her messy hair on my white pillowcases, she just looks so fucking beautiful. I rub my cock against the wetness of her hole and then slide it between her lips to tease her throbbing clit. She moans again, her legs spreading for me. Inviting me in bare.

"Rosa, your body was made for me," I mutter.

Her body arches up off the bed, begging for more. I'm about to plunge deep inside of her when my bedroom door slings open, then slams shut. I launch myself to my bedside table, snatch my .50 caliber Desert Eagle, and swing it toward the door.

"We need to go. Now, *jefe*," Marco Antonio grunts, his eyes sliding behind me, ignoring my gun pointed right at his chest. He clenches his jaw in irritation and it pisses me off. Who I fuck—or almost fuck in this case—is my business.

"Oh, God," Rosa murmurs, yanking the sheet around her. I get a flash of her bare ass as she runs from the room, pushing past my cockblocking friend.

"I'm taking you out tonight, *mami*," I call after her as I set my gun back down. "Be ready because I'll be coming for you."

When she's gone, I let out a groan and saunter over to my dresser to pull out some boxers. Once my erection is no longer flopping around, I turn and glare at him. "What the fuck is so important that you interrupt my Sunday morning with a beautiful woman?"

"She's bad news," he warns.

I stalk into my closet, ignoring him. "Am I going to get bloody?"

"Don't wear your Versace."

I yank a pair of jeans off a hanger and a black T-shirt. After I'm dressed, I throw on some black steel-toed boots and grab my gun to tuck into the back of my jeans. "Give me five minutes to take a piss and brush my teeth."

We cruise along the road in Marco Antonio's black Land Rover to the shed. The rain hasn't let up so the windshield wipers are on full blast, making a hypnotic song. Arturo has three of Guerrero's biggest gangsters in custody. They're with the Osos. Aldo Mendez is organizing this gang into something much bigger, much faster than I can deconstruct the crime gangs around him. He's slick and for some fucking reason, his men are loyal. We may not have Mendez, but we have three of his most trusted men.

We pull up beside Arturo's charcoal-gray Dodge Challenger and I let out a laugh. "Do I want to know how he managed to get all three here in that?"

"Arturo is resourceful, you know this." Boy do I. That's why he's one of my best men. Arturo finds ways to get what I need. He's the people person. Our finder. The fucker makes magic happen. Like a hound, he sniffs them all out and brings them back to his master like a good dog.

I push in the code and follow the screams. They all blend together when we get a bunch of live ones at once. The door to the torture room is ajar and when I open it, I've stepped right into a scene from a horror film.

Velez with balls purple as fuck sits in the middle of the room, eyes wide as he stares at Arturo. Like a good man, Arturo left Velez alone aside from a few twists on his balls. But the others...he's pulling information out like he's been trained to do.

All three detainees are naked and hanging upside down by their ankles from chains attached to the rafters of the building. Men are more vulnerable naked. Plus, it gives us easy access to fuck them up however we need to. The gangster on the far right is either passed out or dead. I'm going with the latter. His inner thigh has been sliced open and blood runs down his chest and face. It drips from his hair onto the floor, making a puddle. The middle gangster is swinging in a circle as he unsuccessfully tries to free himself. And the gangster on the far left is crying. He's young, probably nineteen or twenty.

"Hose," I bark out to Marco Antonio.

He walks over to the hose wrapped up on the wall and turns the water on. Once he's stretched it back over to me, I hold the trigger and aim it at the kid. The water blasts on and I aim for his balls. He screams in pain and tries to cover himself there, so I spray his eyes. When he lets out another wail, I send a spray of water right down his gullet. He gags and chokes. I release the trigger and walk over to him.

"Where's Mendez?"

Vomit spews out of him and lands on my shoe. I'm glad I wore my boots. Once he's done gagging and spitting, I rap my knuckles on his abdomen.

"Where's Mendez?" I ask again.

"Don't tell him, Angel," the middle guy hisses.

"Shut up," I snap at him.

He starts hissing a bunch of curse words. I've had enough of this fucker already. Stalking over to him, I grab a handful of his hair and yank him to me. "Hold him," I bark out.

Marco Antonio holds his arms behind his back and Arturo pries the fuck's mouth open. I shove the metal gun of my water hose into his mouth as deep as I can until he gags. I pull the trigger. He jolts and spazzes as water shoots down the back of his throat. I spray until I think he might drown and then I pull it from his mouth. Water mixed with blood rushes back out and soaks the floor below. He chokes and his body shakes violently. Dark red blood runs from his lips and out his nose. The dick is as good as dead because I've probably just exploded his damn stomach. It doesn't matter, though. I'll get info from Angel.

Turning back to the wide-eyed kid, I hold up the gun of the hose. "Ready to talk?"

"Y-Yes. He's sticking to the north side of the city. Club Cielo," he sputters out.

Interesting development.

Velez starts whimpering. Fucker knows what's coming.

I drop the hose to the floor and storm over to Velez. He smells like a goddamned pig having shit himself. I refuse to clean him off. He can sit in his filth. I stand in front of him and raise my boot.

"N-No! N-No! D-Don't!"

Ignoring him, I smash his purple bulging balls with the toe of my boot. He screams like a fucking woman who's getting her head sawed off. Fucking pussy. With his balls in this precarious position, it wouldn't take much pressure before his skin would split and free them from his sack like a couple of egg yolks tossed into a bowl.

I let up slightly and glower at him. "You played me, motherfucker."

"It wasn't like that," he lies. "I was going to get 'em for you."

Marco Antonio snorts. Arturo laughs. Velez is so full of shit.

"You were told to put the heat on Club Cielo. Get

that shit shut down. Drive that asshole from his nest." I press against his sack again, reveling in his scream. "But you disobeyed me."

I yank my knife from my pocket and flip it open. He starts sobbing, but it does nothing to me. I don't feel sorry for this sick fuck. He's a traitor and a pedo. I grab his chin and hold him still as I carve an E and then an M into his forehead.

El Malo.

When I want to send a message to fuckers like Mendez, I litter the streets with the corpses of his men signed with a warning.

Blood runs down over Velez's eyes and down his cheeks, mixing with his tears. He's so pathetic. Disgusting.

"J-Just kill me," he begs.

I'll do nothing of the sort. Instead of granting him his wish, I whistle as I give his nuts a reprieve and go hunting in the tool box for my thin nylon rope. Arturo picks up on the song and starts singing along as I whistle it. A couple of *baddies* as Rosa says who can carry a fucking tune. Velez eyes the rope warily. He ought to be scared. I squat in front of him, ignoring his stank, and grab hold of his little pecker. Maybe it's a physiological response or maybe he's truly gay, but either way, his cock responds and hardens.

"Our little masochist here wants me to tug on his dick," I tell my men. They both snort in amusement. "Let me oblige, Mayor." I tie one end of the rope around his cock. I tighten the knot enough that I'm sure it really fucking hurts. He passes out, his head lolling back. I stand and toss the other end of the rope over the rafters.

Once I grab the end of it, I tie it around his wrist with his arm stretched above his head.

"Wake up," I order and slap his cheek.

He blinks in confusion and then realizes his situation with horror. "No…"

"Oh, yes," I say with a grin and head over to the sink.

His arm is stretched in the air, but eventually it will get weak and heavy. And when it falls, it'll yank on his cock. If his arm gives out altogether, his cock is going to stretch to a painful limit. He quickly realizes this and lets out a howl.

"Arturo," I holler. "You got this?"

"*Sí, jefe.*" He nods. "I'll extract everything I can from the kid."

"Get me everything you can. I'm going to pay Mendez a visit tonight."

Capítulo Nueve

Rosa

I have a thundering headache and a mountain of regret. But she's home. Araceli walked in just as I finished my shift looking surprisingly refreshed. She assured me Marco Antonio wasn't cruel to her. He took her to a safe house and interrogated her about me and Julio and what happened. Then, he took care of her until she was ready to come back.

After all four of us gushed over her return, I took her back to my room. She thanked me and promised me she was fine. I have no choice but to believe her.

"These," Yolanda says as she reenters my room. Since we're close in size, she's taken it upon herself to be my personal stylist. The moment she found out Javier was taking me out, I thought she was going to faint. She hands me a pair of big gold hoops.

"I can't wear these," I whine. "They're as big as my head."

She laughs and ignores my protests as she sets to putting them in my ears. "It will draw his eyes to your neck." After she gets them in, she lifts a questioning brow at me. "Have you slept with him?"

"Yolanda!" I cry out, embarrassment heating my flesh.

She shrugs. "We're girlfriends. I know you're our boss, but you're like a big sister to us. Spill the details."

My heart clenches in my chest. Truth be told, I've enjoyed letting her fix my hair and apply my makeup. It's one of the most normal things I've ever done in my life. I'm so abnormal, it feels strange to be normal. I've spent so much time with vengeance in my future that I haven't stopped to enjoy the little things in the present. Like letting one of your girlfriends doll you up before a date.

"We haven't even kissed." I bite on my bottom lip.

"But," she urges.

"But we've done other stuff," I whisper. "Don't tell the other girls."

She smiles. "Your secret is safe with me. Does he have a big cock?"

A flush spreads over my skin. I'd gotten a glimpse of his cock this morning and also felt it as it rubbed against me. My job was to seduce him, but in reality, he's the one who seduced me. "Of course he does. You can't be someone like Javier Estrada and not back up that attitude and power with something worthwhile."

"Did he go down on you?"

I close my eyes, but then I'm right there. With his hot breath tickling my center. Quickly, I pop my eyes open. "Yes."

"Oh, God, you lucky bitch. He's so dreamy."

I want to chide her and remind her he's a criminal, but I won't expose myself even to her. "Very dreamy." He's a dreamy bad guy, that much I can admit.

"You're going to have sex with him tonight. Did you

shave your pussy cat?"

Laughing, I nod my head. "I'm good," I assure her. "And why are you so sure I'll have sex with him?" The thought makes my core throb. He's the enemy and I have butterflies dancing in my belly at the thought of getting naked with him again.

"He's taking you on a date, Rosa. He likes you. But he isn't the type of man to not follow through all the way. You're getting laid."

"Maybe," I say with a sigh. I walk over to the full-length mirror and hardly recognize myself. Yolanda lent me a white bandage dress that's not only short but extremely fitted. It's low cut and shows off everything. Cleavage. My curvy hips. Toned thighs. She's curled my dark, chocolate-colored hair into loose beach waves that hang down in front of my shoulders. But it's my face I hardly recognize. She's given me fake lashes that make my eyelashes seem thicker and fuller and painted my lips matte red. I look like a movie star.

"Hot damn, *mami*. You're looking so fine tonight." Javier's deep voice rumbles from the doorway.

I jerk my head his way and my mouth goes dry. He wears a pair of light gray slacks and a white button-up shirt. The top two buttons have been left undone, giving him a slightly casual look, especially with the way the sleeves are rolled partway up his arms. His gold watch is big and shiny, catching the overhead light and glimmering. I bet it costs more than any of his cars. Javier loves fashion. The ink on his forearms snakes out past the material and gives a sharp contrast to his sleek outfit. Dangerous yet impeccable. If his style had a name it'd be villain chic. His belt is black and has a texture like maybe snakeskin. On his feet, he wears a pair of shiny black dress shoes. When my eyes make their way back to his, he's grinning at me, an incredibly hot dimple making itself known.

"You look pretty fine yourself," I murmur, a genuine smile tugging at my lips.

Yolanda laughs but then slips out of the room, leaving us alone. Like a jaguar in the jungle, he prowls my way. His hands find my hips and I shiver.

"As much as I want to throw you down on your bed and have my way with you, I promised you a night out," he utters, his thumbs running circles on my hips.

I gaze up at him, enjoying being the center of his attention. I'd thought seducing this man would be difficult. Turns out, it's the easiest thing I've ever done.

Because he's seducing you, Rosa…

Since we're dressed nice, I expect to go eat at one of the fancy hotels along the ocean—one of the few undisturbed by crime places left in Acapulco. Instead, he drives me to the heart of the city. His men ride behind us in Marco Antonio's Land Rover, but Javier is driving us in his 1957 cherry-red Chevrolet Thunderbird. It's been completely restored and I've never been so in love with a car before. The radio plays a new up-and-coming Mexican band and Javier taps on the steering wheel as he sings along.

I can't stop staring at him.

For a bad guy, he's the most beautiful man I've ever seen.

His black hair is styled in a tousled way and he's left some black scruff on his cheeks rather than shaving. My palms itch to run my fingers along his sharp jawline and down his neck that's corded with lean muscle.

The rain patters on the car, but Javier isn't bothered as he weaves through the streets as though he comes this way all the time. It makes me realize how sheltered I've been due to my job. Michael has made it clear that my job was to remain on the estate and to not venture out into the dangerous city. Whenever we'd go out to dinner, it was always someplace we could walk to and bring back to the hotel room. I'm now passing buildings I've never seen before. Even in the rain, with them all lit up, it's beautiful. We pull up to a building that has people standing outside the door with umbrellas waiting.

"They look too busy," I say, a slight pout to my voice when I realize it's a restaurant.

"Not too busy for an Estrada," he replies cockily. He climbs out of the car where Arturo waits with an umbrella. When my car door opens, Javier stands beside it with his arm outstretched and the other one holding an umbrella. I accept his hand and he pulls me close to him to protect me from the rain. It's hard to remember sometimes that he's evil personified. A murdering leader of a Mexican cartel. Él es el malo. *He is the bad guy.* But with his strong arm wrapped around my waist and smelling like heaven as he behaves as a perfect gentleman, I find the line blurring for me.

Michael never opened doors for me.

Not even back in Virginia where we met. Then, it was always drinks after work and I'd end up in his bed. In the beginning, our relationship was hot and had hope for a future. But about six months after coming to Acapulco, he changed. Started drinking more. Keeping me at arm's length when it came to emotions. Fucking me as though it was his right, but he didn't even seem to enjoy it half the time.

Javier's fingers tighten around my waist when we pass a guy who eyeballs my tits in the dress. He walks us past the line and into the dark, tiny restaurant. As soon as he closes the umbrella, an old man with a mustache rushes over to him.

"Javier, *mijo!*" the old man greets with a wide grin. "*Siéntate con tu bella dama.*" *Come sit with your beautiful lady.*

"*Gracias*, Jorge," Javier says and flashes me a smug grin as we follow the old man.

"*¡Levántense!*" Jorge orders a couple of teenage boys when we reach a table near the back.

The boys groan and leave, carrying their plates with them. Jorge produces a wet cloth from his belt and quickly cleans the table as if two seconds ago people weren't just dining there. This place reminds me of my favorite restaurant and the old man treats Javier like Ana treated me.

Like family.

Pain crushes my heart as I take my seat. I can't look at him. I'll see their eyes. The ones who stormed in and shot up everyone I cared about. He is the enemy. I need to remember that.

"*Dos margaritas de cocos,*" Javier says to Jorge. His tone sounds dismissive. "Rosa." He grabs my hand and I wince. "What is it? Do you want to go somewhere nicer?"

My eyes sting with tears and I blink rapidly to rid them. "N-No. This is perfect. Just reminded me of a restaurant I used to eat at as a girl in Ciudad Juárez." I lift my gaze to find him staring intensely at me. The slivers of light brown in his dark eyes seems to brighten and flicker with worry. "I'm fine," I assure him. "I just really miss their *tacos al pastor*." That's not a lie.

He studies me for a minute before he reaches for the menus tucked behind the salt and pepper shakers and about seven different types of hot sauces. This place is kind of dingy and old, but it's perfect. It even smells like my childhood.

"Lucky for you," he tells me, his eyes narrowed as if he's watching my every facial tick and blink. "They have the best *tacos al pastor* in all of Mexico."

I lift a brow. "I doubt it could beat Miguel's. He was the master."

"Was?"

Swallowing, I throw him a bone. One thing we learned in training was that you give them nibbles of the truth so that when you deliver your lies, they flow more easily from you.

"He was killed," I tell him softly. "Gangsters he owed money to."

The tense moment is interrupted when Jorge sets down two giant margarita glasses. They each have a skewer sticking out of them with cut bananas, strawberries, and fat marshmallows. I've never seen a drink like this before.

"*Rosa no cree que sirvas los mejores tacos al pastor en México,*" Javier tattles, a playful grin back on his handsome face. *Rosa does not think you serve the best tacos al pastor in Mexico.*

"I didn't say that," I argue.

Jorge puffs out his chest and waggles his meaty finger at me. *"Verás, bella dama."* He storms off as though he's on a mission. *You will see, beautiful lady.*

"I can't believe you told him that," I say with a groan as someone sets some chips and salsa down in front of us. My stomach grumbles in appreciation. I pick up a tortilla chip and dip it. "He'll probably poison us now."

He pulls his gun from his back and sets it on the table. "Jorge knows better than to fuck with El Malo."

I glance around the bustling restaurant and nobody notices his chrome and black, long barreled Desert Eagle. One glance tells me it's .50 caliber. Same one he pulled on Marco Antonio this morning. They hold seven rounds.

"They don't care," he assures me. "But you do. Are you familiar with guns?" His probe sends my heart rate skyrocketing.

"I've shot them before," I tell him before taking a sip of the light brown margarita. It's heavy on the tequila but tastes really good.

"Full of surprises, *manzanita.*"

I flash him a quick smile and change the subject. "When will Sr. Estrada arrive?"

A smile, filled with love and respect tugs at his lips. "Father and Tania will be here Friday." He sips his margarita. "We're having a party Friday night."

Normally, when he has parties, we prepare all the food but then are to stay out of the way. I wonder if this still applies to me.

"I want you there," he says, his voice dark and dripping with intent. "Do you have a swimsuit? The weather will be nice by then."

"No, I don't have much, but maybe I can borrow one—"

"When we get home, use my computer to order whatever you need." His eyes narrow at me. "The password is candyapple."

I swallow down another sip of my strong margarita. I'm trying to keep the satisfied look off my face. If I have access to his computer, there's no telling what I could uncover for the agency. This whole seduction operation is giving us more progress and access than we've had the entire four years I've been here. Michael was right. This is working.

"Thank you," I say.

While we wait on our food, he pulls his pack of little cigars out and lights one. He leans back in his chair, his sharp and hungry gaze boring into me. I feel like this date is a test and if I can pass it, he'll let me into his world.

I can do this.

"You're beautiful," he tells me.

Heat floods my cheeks and I fight a smile. "You're a romantic, Javi."

His eyes lazily slide to my lips, down my throat, and settle on my cleavage. He exhales a plume of sweet smelling smoke and it clouds the air around us. I feel as though he's creating this bubble for us—an intoxicating haze I'll never be able to climb my way out of. With his intense inspection, I find myself fidgeting under his stare. He brings his cigar back to his lips and sucks, his scruffy cheeks pulling in. His full lips part and the smoke pours out like a snake slithering out of its trap. It slides my way and swirls around me.

Only Javier Estrada could make smoking little candy apple cigars look so hot.

"You're blushing, *mami*."

I laugh. "You're practically making love to your cigar."

His grin is immediate and I'm rewarded with the dimple I'm growing quite fond of. "I'm good with my mouth as you well know."

I bite on my lip and relax in my seat. Despite charming the enemy, this is kind of fun. I'd never tell Michael that. You won't find on any of the reports to the CIA that I enjoyed a date with one of Mexico's most nefarious men. That I let him stick his tongue inside me. His finger in my ass. They'd pull me and send me back to Virginia faster than I could blink.

"You were okay," I tease.

His eyes darken as he leans forward, his little cigar stuck between his teeth. Damn, he's hot. Too hot. I'm going to fuck everything up because of this man. He gets inside my head and makes me forget who I am.

"Should I drag you across this table, spread you right open, and feast upon your sweet cunt again to remind you that I am *better* than okay?" He smirks and then takes another drag on his cigar. "We both know I was your motherfucking best."

With those words, he blows the sweet smoke at me before leaning back in his chair. Jorge arrives with several dishes and I don't even have to dig in to know this food will be better than anything I've ever tasted.

Javier stubs out his cigar and we eat, discussing some musicians we both like. He keeps the margaritas coming. Once I'm stuffed and tipsy, he throws down some money, shoves his Desert Eagle back into his pants, and helps me to my feet. I stumble, not quite used to the high heels, and he pulls me to his chest. My thigh rubs against his and something metal is smashed between us.

"Are you happy to see me?" I tease, tilting my head up to look at him.

His palms find my ass and he squeezes. "Give me some credit, *manzanita*. Surely you don't confuse my switchblade for my big cock. Do you remember the way I rubbed against you this morning?" He nuzzles his face against my hair near my ear. "You were so wet for me."

I still am.

Heat floods through me and I want to beg him to take me home now. I'm seconds away from mauling him in front of everyone at this busy restaurant. He chuckles and pulls away before guiding me outside and into the rain where his men wait. Marco Antonio walks us to Javier's car that sits in the same place we left it. He gets soaked while he makes sure we stay dry. Being with Javier is like being with a prince. A dark, fucked up prince, but still a prince. He has men who bow to him. An entire city of people who quake in fear of making him angry.

Once we're settled in the car, his hand seeks out my bare thigh and he squeezes me there. The small act of affection has me desperate to return it. I slide my palm over his. He darts his gaze my way, studying me like he always does.

"You're beautiful, Rosa."

I give him a thankful smile. Javier may be a lot of bad things but he's good things too, and complimentary is one of them. He says such sweet, seductive things to me. And what he doesn't say, his body language does for him. His hungry stares. The way he prowls toward me whenever I'm near.

He turns his palm up and I slide my fingers to interlink with his. Satisfied at holding my hand, he settles in his seat as he maneuvers the streets. His head moves to the beat and he taps the steering wheel along with the drums in the song. This man loves his music.

"Club Cielo," he says as we pull into a spot. The rain continues to pour, but we're not letting it put a damper on things. "I want you to have some fun and then I have business to take care of here."

A cold dose of reality drenches me, sobering me up some.

I'm here to spy.

Not turn into a girly pile of goo who's enjoying the best date of her life.

Focus, Daza, focus.

"Of course, baddie," I tease, despite the strain in my voice.

Always so in tune to me, he senses it. "You know who I am," he reminds me.

Nodding, I stare out the windshield to the sleek club. "El Malo."

He leans my way and slides a hand into my hair. I gasp when he pulls me to him. His lips that smell of tequila are close to mine but not close enough to touch. "We're going to dance, we're going to drink, and we're going to have a good time. I'll take care of business on the way out." He runs his thumb along my jawline. "And then when I get you home, Rosa, I'm going to fuck you. I'm going to fuck you and stake my claim on whatever it is that's happening between us."

"Okay," I breathe out in agreement. He could ask for anything right now and I'd say yes as long as he gives me the kiss I ache for.

His fingers slide to the back of my skull and he grips my hair almost to the point of pain. He clutches my throat with his other hand. "I'm greedy, *manzanita*. When I want something, I find a way to have it. I will have it. And as you know, I take care of my things once I get them." He doesn't choke me, simply holds me in an almost reverent way. "If you're not ready for me to suck you into my world, you need to back out right the fuck now."

I part my lips and meet his blazing gaze. "You'd let me climb out of this car and walk away if I said I didn't want to be sucked in?"

His lips quirk up on one side. "Fuck no. You're already here. You belong to El Malo now, so deal with it." And with those words, he presses his soft lips to mine. I let out an appreciative moan that gives him access to my mouth with his insistent tongue. He swipes it across mine and I'm already drunk off him. One simple taste and I need more. So much more. I kiss him back hungrily, my palms seeking out his muscled shoulders. I want to touch him like he touches me. Everywhere. Possessively. All at once. Our tongues duel for the lead, but he wins because he involves his teeth. Reminds me he's the powerful one here. I cry out when he nips at my tongue. His palm slides down my throat and along my chest until he has my breast in his hand. Each place he touches burns as though his hands are on fire. I *want* him to burn me.

I'm dizzy and drunk for him.

I try to climb into his lap, but we're interrupted by a

rap on the glass.

"For fuck's sake, Marco," he roars.

I shrink away back to my seat. My door opens and Arturo stands ready with an umbrella. Marco Antonio and Javier are in a yelling match that sounds like it might end with a fist to the face, but Javier storms away from him in the pouring rain. His Desert Eagle gets pulled from his back and my heart rate quickens. But he doesn't fire it. Instead, he jerks his shirt untucked and hides it in the back of his pants again. He yanks the umbrella from Arturo's grip and holds it over me as we walk inside. The sweet romancer from moments ago has morphed into this raging demon.

It's just the wakeup call I needed.

Capítulo Diez

Javier

Marco Antonio is going to get his ass kicked before the night is over. We may be friends and he may feel like a brother to me, but he needs to learn to not fuck with me when I'm with Rosa. It's like he's trying to sabotage our moments on purpose. I know he doesn't like her and has his suspicions, but it's not his place. When it comes to her, I know what I'm doing, goddammit.

She's nervous, no longer the woman who was practically melting in my car. Now, she's alert and rigid. We may be walking into Aldo Mendez's stomping ground, but these people are afraid of me. And if his men try anything, my guys will slaughter them all before they even have a chance to come at me.

The music is loud and the club is full. It's close to the hotels, so there are some American tourists here. Annoying as fuck but nothing I can do about it. If they knew what was good for them, they'd take their asses back to their resort where they belong. They're on El Malo and Osos's battlefield and they don't even realize it.

I escort Rosa over to the bar and motion to the

expensive bottle of Don Julio on the top shelf. The bartender, wise to who I am, reaches up and pours two shots without so much as a question if I can afford it. I hand one to Rosa, and together, we knock them back. Whatever has her tense as fuck begins to loosen its hold by the third shot. She starts dancing in place and I watch her in amusement. Something catches my eye and Arturo is behind her.

"He's here," he mouths.

I nod as I take another shot. Once Rosa has had hers, I grab her wrist and tug her onto the busy dance floor. We push past some sweaty bodies until we find a place to dance. I twist her in my arms and pull her back flush against my chest. Her hips start moving to the rhythm, her round ass rubbing against my cock that's been hard for her since this morning when I was fucking her with my tongue. I move with her, learning her pattern quickly, and let my palms roam up her ribs. She collects her hair in her hands and lifts it off her sweaty neck and flashes me a hungry look. I run my palms down past the material of her dress to her thighs and inch it up. Her head tilts back and slides to the side, inviting me in.

"Oh, *mami*, you look good enough to eat," I say loudly near her ear so she'll hear over the music. Then, I run my tongue up the side of her sweaty neck. Her salty taste makes me want to lick it all from her. She drops her hair and one hand comes up behind her to cup the back of my neck. I bite on her flesh and suck it hard, my intent to mark her for everyone to see. Every asshole who's been eyefucking her since we walked in can see she is with me. She is El Malo now. Marco Antonio can have his reservations, but I don't give a fuck. I want her and nothing will stop me from having her.

She twists around and wraps her arms around my neck, her body never stopping its sensual dancing. I grab her hips and pull her against me, my dick hard between us. The lust swimming in her eyes is something I could get high from. Leaning forward, I nip at her bottom lip and grab the back of her thigh, lifting her leg to my waist. I maneuver myself so my hard cock through my clothes rubs against where she's no doubt dripping for me. Her eyes flutter and her head tilts back.

Goddammit, she's gorgeous.

I grind against her and bite her chin and jaw and throat. With our clothes fully on, I dry-fuck her right in front of everyone. I own her cunt and stake a mother-fucking claim. Her tits jiggle as I thrust against her. She tenses for a second before an orgasm shudders through her. Several grungy guys nearby are watching with salacious grins on their faces. I glower at them to look the fuck away. They must see my hate and fury for anything other than the woman who's in my arms because they back away and look elsewhere.

As soon as she calms, I ease her leg back down and kiss her nose.

"Water," she croaks.

I laugh at her but then shoot each male in the vicinity a warning glare before pretending to pop each one of them in the skull. If that isn't a warning that I'm packing and I'll put them down like dogs, I don't know what is. An American woman with red curly hair walks up to Rosa and starts dancing. I figure she's safe enough and Alejandro is only a few feet away. Stalking over to the bar, I see Marco Antonio in a discussion with Arturo. Once I have her glass of water in hand, I walk over to them.

"Mendez is pissed, *jefe*," Marco Antonio barks out. "Saw him and a couple of his guys watching you with your girl on the dance floor."

My girl. About time he starts to get that through his thick skull. Earlier, in the parking lot, I was about to deck him for warning me about her for the fiftieth god-damned time. I know what the fuck I'm doing and it doesn't concern him.

"Let him be pissed," I snarl. "I'm pissed he thinks he can undo everything I've done. He answers to El Malo. Guerrero answers to El Malo."

With that, I storm back over to *my girl.* But when I'm about six feet away, I stop dead in my tracks. Motherfucking Aldo Mendez with his shaved tattooed head is dancing with *my girl* in his arms. Unlike five min-utes prior where she enjoyed the hell out of our danc-ing, she's stiff and nervous. She doesn't want that ass-hole touching her.

I don't want that piece of shit touching her.

"Rosa," I bellow, my voice carrying over the music.

She starts to pull away and his tattooed-covered hand gropes her tit. Red. I see motherfucking red. He glares at me over her head, his spider web tattoos all over his face making him look like some kind of fuck-ing demon. I smash the water glass by slamming it to the floor.

"Let go," she cries out and elbows him hard in the stomach, knocking the breath out of him. Then, she lifts her leg and kicks behind her, aiming for his balls. Her foot hits its intended target because he stumbles back-ward. She starts for me when I see him reach into the waistband of his jeans. I pull out my switchblade and pop it out as I charge past her. I'm on him in no time, my hand gripping his arm and forcing it up toward the ceiling. He fires off one, two, three shots and people start screaming and running.

"You do not fucking touch what's mine!" I roar as I ram the knife into his right side and then drag it all the way across his abdomen to the other side. His eyes are wild as he stares into the orbs of the devil himself. I hope he spends the rest of eternity wherever he ends up with my hateful face on loop in his mind.

You don't fucking touch Javier Estrada's property.

He chokes and his gun falls to the ground.

With my left hand, I shove my hand into his now gaping stomach and grab onto whatever I can get my hands on. Hot, meaty organs are in my grip. As I pull at them, I hike my foot up and kick his hip, sending him jerking backward. His entrails are yanked straight from his body and he falls to the floor as useless as the day he was born. Except now, he's not kicking or screaming, he's fucking still.

Pop! Pop! Pop!

I twist around, the dead fuck's innards still in my fist, and lock eyes with the wide ones of Rosa. My men have their guns raised and several bodies litter the floor. People have scattered and the music no longer plays.

"He fucked with El Malo!" I yell to anyone who will listen. I slam the guts to the floor with a messy splatter and stalk back over to his corpse. I carve an E and an M in his forehead and do the same with the men my guys took down. By the time I'm finished, I'm covered in sticky blood. I fold my knife up and shove it in my pocket.

Rosa doesn't cower when I stride over to her and snag her delicate wrist with my bloodstained hand. I clutch her neck and draw her to me so my hot breath that's rushing out in heavy pants comingles with her.

"No one touches you but me," I growl.

My lips smash to hers and I kiss her hard. I claim her in front of those who are left. Nobody calls the police because they won't come anyway. Acapulco, Guerrero, is under my reign now. She whimpers and I realize my grip has tightened on her throat. I slide my hand to the tit Aldo Mendez just had a hold of and I smear his blood all over her white dress. She kisses me harder and more desperately. I grab her ass with both hands and pick her up. With her in my grip and her legs wrapped around my waist, I carry her through the emptying club and out into the pouring rain.

"I'm going to fuck you," I tell her as I walk along the side of the building.

The moment I reach the corner, I walk us between the two buildings. Rain pelts us and she shivers in my arms.

"I'm going to warm you up, *mami*," I tell her. "Now take my cock out."

As she unzips my zipper and reaches into my boxers, I groan at having her small hand wrapped around my thickness. I lean her against the wall and jerk her dress up to her hips. The rain is unrelenting, soaking us to the bone, but neither of us seems to care. Her fingers grip at her thong and she pulls it aside. I hiss as she guides me where she wants me.

"*Eres mía*," I growl against her cold lips as I push

into her tight heat. "Do you hear me, *manzanita*? You're mine."

She nods and clutches onto my shoulders. "*Sí*, Javi!"

I thrust my hips hard against her. Her screams are ones of pleasure and I want to taste them. My lips find hers and I own her with a kiss as I fuck her against the brick wall. I've never had the desire to completely own someone before. I want to mark her up and force everyone to see who she belongs to.

I'm fucked in the head because of this woman.

I suck on her tongue and then start kissing along her cheek to her ear, whispering praises so soft I wonder if she even hears. But based on the way her cunt clenches with each adoring word, I know she does. Rosa Delgado needs to be worshipped by a king. She may be a sexy maid and I a glorified gangster, but together we make the world tremble beneath our feet as though we're gods put on the earth to rule the lesser thans. Because, after all, they're all lesser than compared to the likes of my sweet Rosa.

She cries out, her nails digging into my shoulders. I bury my face into her rain-soaked hair as I drive into her. Her big as fuck earring is in the way, so I kiss around it and whisper more dirty things into her ear. Her pussy clenches and she shudders, an orgasm taking over. I close my eyes and press my lips to her cheek near her ear as I fuck her furiously. With a savage growl, I come. Her name is trickled from my lips as I spill my seed into her needy cunt.

"Pull out," she whines. "Javi, pull out."

I bite her throat and drain the rest of my climax into her. "I can't pull out when you say my name like that, *mami*. I'm too high on you." I lick the rain from her neck and then pull away to look at her.

Her eyes are wide and filled with shame. Fuck that. I kiss her hard on the mouth until she relaxes in my arms. Eventually, I pull away and lean my forehead against hers.

"Rosa, you're mine. In case you didn't hear the first time…"

She furls her eyebrows together. "I heard you."

Heard me, but she doesn't believe me.

I'll get through to her one way or another.

Even if I have to brand my goddamned name on her.

She. Will. Eventually. Understand.

By the time we make it home, we're waterlogged. She starts for her room, but I don't let her go. We look fucking awful. She's missing one of her fake eyelashes and her mascara is smeared down her face. I'm covered in blood and my bloody handprints are all over her dress. I scoop her light frame into my arms and stalk through the house to my bedroom.

"You're making such a mess," she complains.

"Maybe the hot maid will clean it up tomorrow," I tease.

She cracks a smile and I love it. Her smiles, which I learn are fairly rare, are like smoking weed. They just fill you up and make you horny as fuck. I'm high just looking at her. Once in my massive bathroom, I set her to her feet and step into my marbled shower and turn it on. With two shower heads up top and two that spray from the wall, it's the best damn shower in the world. I turn to see her hugging her middle. Too late to be apprehensive now. I've jumped in with both feet just like when I cliff dive at La Quebrada. It's a risky jump and you plunge deep, but it's so worth the adrenaline rush.

I stalk my woman. When I reach her, she won't meet my gaze. I grip her chin with my thumb and finger, tilting her head up. "Too late to back out now."

"I'm not backing out," she murmurs. Her lip trembles. "I'm just scared."

"Of me, *manzanita*?"

Tears well in her eyes. "Of everything."

I press a kiss to her plump lips. "I'll protect you from all of it."

"Who will protect me from you?" A single tear rolls out.

My hands slide to her shoulders and I peel her dress down, baring her breasts to me. "No one will protect you. I'm going to take you and use you and own you. Mine, *mami*."

"You barely know me," she murmurs.

I drag her dress down over her hips and let it fall to the floor. Her panties get pushed down next. She steps out of her shoes, pulls off her other false eyelash, and then tugs off the big hoop earrings from her ears as I fly through the buttons on my shirt. I toss it to the floor and put my Desert Eagle on the granite countertop. Reaching behind me, I grip my undershirt behind my neck and peel it off me. Her eyes slide to my chest and she stares at my ink as I unbuckle my belt. I lose the rest of my clothes and hold my hand that's stained with blood out to her. She hesitates for a moment before sliding her hand into mine. I lead her into the shower under the hot spray.

I clean off that motherfucker's blood while she watches with the saddest eyes I've ever seen. Once I'm clean, I wash her. Slowly and gently. Being with someone like me isn't easy. You'll be forced to give up everything. When I want something, I want all of it. I don't want to share it with anyone. Father spoiled me, what can I say?

I squirt some shampoo into my palm and start washing her long locks. Her lids flutter closed and she parts her lips. My cock is hard between our slick-from-soap bodies and her firm tits rub against my chest. I'll be inside of her soon enough. Until then, I'll enjoy taking care of her. And as much as I like showering her with attention, she fucking eats it up. Tentatively, she wraps her arms around my back and leans her cheek against me.

"You barely know me," she repeats, "yet here you are making vows with someone you don't even know."

I smirk and fist her hair before twisting it. Pulling down, I force her to look up at me. "I know everything I need to know." I lean my forehead against hers. "The rest we'll fill in along the way."

She doesn't seem convinced, but she does relax. After a long shower, I hand her a towel. I'm not done with her tonight. She needs to chill the fuck out and I know just the way. Hand in hand, I guide her over to my French doors. My deck faces the ocean but is covered from the elements. I walk over to the hot tub and flip the top open. It's hot, but I want it hotter. I turn the dial and push the button to turn on the jets.

"Get in," I tell her. "I'll be right back."

She nods and drops her towel. I watch her ass jiggle as she climbs the steps. Her butt is big in comparison to the rest of her body and I love the way it moves. I fucking love there's a lot to grab on to. My cock twitches beneath my towel. Ignoring it for now, I walk inside and locate a Xanax for her and a bottle of Casa Dragones Blue Agave tequila for me.

"Here," I say as I saunter over to the hot tub.

She frowns but opens her mouth like a good girl. I push the pill onto her tongue.

"Drink it down with this." I unscrew the cap and hand her the bottle.

After she swallows it down, I lose the towel and join her. I take a pull from the tequila and then set it on the edge. Since the night is cool, the hot tub is extra steamy.

"Come here," I order, pulling her into my lap.

Once she realizes I'm only wanting to hold her, she settles against me. Her body relaxes in my arms.

"Let me tell you what I know," I say as I stroke her back beneath the water. "I know you have excellent taste in music and can dance like you were born to do it. I know you love Jorge's *tacos al pastor* the best." She chuckles softly as I continue. "I know your ex, Michael, is a douchebag. I know you are insanely OCD about dust and dirt and wrinkles."

She turns and looks up at me, a smile on her lips. "There's more about me."

Arching a brow at her, I grab her hips and position her to straddle me. "I know you taste like heaven."

"Better than your candy apple cigars?" she challenges, her brown eyes gleaming with happiness.

"Sweeter and much more addictive," I agree. "I know you haven't always been a little maid who sticks to the shadows and cleans my home."

Her body stiffens slightly. "Oh yeah?"

"I know what's important right now," I tell her as I grip my cock that's hardened again. "And right now I know you need me."

She slides down my shaft to the hilt, her tits pressing against my chest.

"I'm going to give you me, *manzanita*. I'm going to give you all of me."

She opens her mouth like she wants to say something, but I grip her neck, pushing her slightly away from me, and grab her tit with the other hand. Lifting her heavy tit, I bring it to my mouth and tease the nipple with the tip of my tongue. Her cunt clenches and I hiss.

"Javi," she murmurs.

"Yes, *mami?*"

"I'm taking the night off." Her words are thick with meaning, as if she means more than her job as my maid. "Now fuck me like you meant everything you just said."

I grin against her breast. "Hang on." I bite her nipple, relishing in her scream of pleasure. "It's going to be a long, wild ride."

Capítulo Once

Rosa

I wake to Javier's lips on my neck and his cock rubbing against me. I don't have time to process what's happening before he's pushing his thickness deep inside me. My fingernails claw his shoulders as he drives into me, his hips seemingly doing a dance against me. I try to grasp onto reasons of why this is a bad idea, but I come up short. His mouth finds mine and he kisses me. Only Javier would taste good early in the morning. Like candy apple tobacco and tequila. I worry for a moment that I'm going to gross him out with my morning breath, but he practically inhales me. His palm squeezes my tit before sliding to my throat. He's gentle as he grips me, not hard enough to cut off my air. It reminds me of his power.

His other hand grabs one of my wrists and pins it to the bed. He lifts up so he can watch me. I stare at him in wonder. The devil is the sexiest man I've ever seen. His black hair is messy and hangs in his eyes. Dark scruff dusts his cheeks and his nearly black eyes flicker with need.

Need for me.

I try to latch on to the whys.

Why I'm here.

Why I'm doing this.

Why I willingly took Xanax when it was offered to me.

Why I've slept with this man several times now, all without protection.

And I can't seem to find the answers.

I'm spiraling.

I'm spinning and he's the one controlling my movement.

"Come for me, *mami*," he rumbles, his sexy voice hoarse from sleep.

He releases my wrist and reaches between us to rub my clit. I've masturbated many times alone in my room, but it has never felt like when Javier touches me. It's like he's read and memorized the manual to my body.

"Oh, God," I whimper.

Stars glitter around me and I let go.

My back arches off the bed, my body shaking with pleasure. I'm so lost in the throes of passion I don't have it in me to fight him when I feel his heat rush into me. Stupid. So stupid. And yet, his promise dances around in my head, taunting me.

He said he'd take care of me.

His cock softens and he pulls out before lying half on me and on the bed beside me. I love his massive weight crushing me. For a short while, I can pretend it's just us. Nothing exists outside his bedroom door. We're lovers on the fast track for more. He's not king of the cartel. I'm not with the CIA.

"You're quiet," he observes.

"Just tired," I lie.

"Hmmmm…"

"There's a lot of work to do before your father arrives. I should go," I tell him.

His cum trickles out of my body and down my ass crack. I should clean myself up. I should do a lot of things.

"Stay in bed, Rosa. The other maids will do the work."

I start to argue but bite my tongue. It benefits my mission for the agency to stay right under his thumb. I'll learn much more than dusting under beds. Not to mention, you don't argue with a man like Javier Estrada.

"Don't you have baddie work to go do?" I tease, hoping to draw out some information.

"I could be good if I got to spend my every waking moment between your thighs, *manzanita*."

I laugh because despite being so cutthroat and ruthless, sometimes he's playful and funny. But then I remember last night. How he sliced that man open and pulled out his guts. I'd been reminded what a monster he truly is. What he's capable of.

"What happens when you get bored of sleeping with me?"

He growls and nips at my collarbone. "I won't get bored. I'm keeping you."

What happens when I gather all the intel the CIA needs? They swoop in and take down Estrada. By what means, I'm not sure. The idea of him face down in the dirt dirtying up one of his fancy suits doesn't sit well with me.

My mother's bloody body is forefront in my mind, though.

Always reminding me.

People like Javier are like the men who killed my mother.

They. Must. Be. Taken. Down.

I'm dragged from my thoughts to find Javier's intense gaze boring into mine. As though he can peer straight into my head and see the thoughts turning. I attempt to calm my features. He reaches up and I try not to flinch. His hand doesn't strike me, but instead his fingers stroke down the side of my face. I close my eyes, leaning into his touch.

This is bad.

So bad.

He gets inside my head so easily and makes a mess of things.

"Today, we'll go shopping. I want to buy you some things," he says as he slides out of the bed.

I watch his toned ass flex as he walks toward the bathroom. His back is completely tattooed and some of the curls from the design dip onto his butt. God, he's so hot.

He reaches the doorway and turns to look at me. His smile is wide, revealing his one dimple. With a motion of his head, he indicates I should follow.

I follow, a grin of my own on my face, because it's my job.

Also, I follow because I'm a woman and good or bad, nobody can turn down a man like that.

I'm fussing over another borrowed outfit from Yolanda when Araceli rushes into my room.

"Miss Rosa," she says, her brows furled together.

"You have a visitor."

My heart catches in my throat. The only time I should ever have a visitor is if they're extricating me before taking Estrada down. But there's no way they have the intel to do something like that right now. Unnerved, I wave her away and hurry downstairs. I make it outside and find Michael standing just inside the gate. He's wearing a baseball cap and a baggy black T-shirt with a pair of khaki shorts. His new rounded stomach stretches the fabric. I'm disgusted that I let this man use me. At least Javier, despite being a monster, treats me like I'm something worthy of his affection and attention.

"Fuck me," he mutters upon seeing me.

I'm wearing an orange halter top dress that hits me just above my knees. It dips down low in the front and reveals a good portion of my breasts. It's sexy and risqué but very much the style of what women wear around here.

"What are you doing here?" I hiss. There are cameras everywhere. One wrong word. One false move. It will all crash down around me.

"I missed you. Come have dinner with me," he pleads. "I'm sorry. I didn't mean what I said. I love you, Rosa."

I'm stunned at his words. The code, if I were to leave that place, was just the first part. But he added the rest, which feels awfully genuine. I think he's just screwing up his cover because he feels like an ass.

"I have dinner plans," I say, my voice cold. That is my code for: Not yet, I'm still working on some good information.

"This isn't about dinner," he grumbles. "It's about us."

He takes a step forward and I take two back.

"There is no us, remember?" My tone is icy. Nothing about my words has anything to do with the CIA and everything to do with how he treated me.

"Rosa…" He trails off as his eyes dart behind me.

A warm body steps behind me and a strong arm wraps around my middle.

"Everything okay here?" Javier rumbles as he kisses the top of my head.

Michael glowers at me, his face turning bright red. I have to fix this before Michael ruins everything or gets himself killed.

"I have dinner plans tonight with Javier, but I will catch up with you on my day off," I tell him, shooting daggers at him. "We're about to leave, so…"

His eyes drop to where Javier holds me possessively and his jaw clenches. "I'm sorry," he utters again. "Saturday sounds good." He turns on his heel and stalks past the open gate to the road.

When he's gone, Javier speaks. "I don't like him."

Turning in his arms, I attempt to distract him. "Do we have to go shopping? Can't we stay here?"

His irritation melts away as he smirks at me. "You can sit on my cock later. I want to buy you some dresses for while my father is visiting. You'll be on my arm as my lover, not as my maid. Understood?"

My cheeks heat, but I nod. "I'm not going to turn down free clothes."

"Who said they're free?" he teases as his palms grip my ass through my dress. He kneads my flesh, spreading my ass cheeks apart, which quickly makes me wet for him.

"What do I have to do for them?" I bite my bottom lip as I slide my palms up his dress shirt. "I should start on my payment plan."

He lifts me and I squeal but in a way that feels natural. I wrap my legs around him. He presses kisses to my exposed flesh as he walks over to the carport. When he sets me down beside a black Challenger, I pout.

"I thought we were going to, you know…"

He throws his head back and laughs, his Adam's apple bobbing in his throat. "*Mami*, you're a temptation. It is so hard to deny you when you hit me with those pouty fucking lips."

"So don't deny me."

He opens the car door and motions for me to sit. "If I gave you what you wanted, I'd never get a damn thing done. Later, I'll be back inside of you. Now, we do some business."

I let out a sigh but sit in the car. He gets in beside me and fires up the loud engine. It's a standard, so he doesn't hold my hand this time. His focus is on shifting gears and maneuvering the streets that are scattered with potholes filled with rainwater from the storm. Thankfully, today, the sun is out and shining. I assume he'll drive us into the city, but he takes us to the shed. This is the second time he's brought me here.

"What's in there?" I ask as we pull up and park.

He flashes me a dark look. "Business."

"I don't want to stay out here alone."

His brows crash together as he considers my words. "I suppose after what you saw last night at the club, nothing should surprise you. You can come with me, just stay clear of the piss puddles."

I inwardly cringe but give him a quick nod. We get out and I follow behind him. He's wearing black slacks and a white dress shirt with his sleeves rolled up. I love that his tattoos are on display. His black hair is slicked back today, giving him a bad boy mobster look. I definitely approve. He keys in the code and I memorize the number. When he pushes into the building, someone wails.

He grabs my hand and pulls me after him. We make it to a room where the noises are coming from. When he opens that door, I'm assaulted with a disgusting smell. The first thing I notice in what looks like a torture room is a man sitting in a chair, his head slumped forward. Naked. He has metal twisted around his balls. I cringe. Another man hangs from the ceiling, his eyes wild but very much alive.

"Rosa, meet Velez and Angel." He points to each one. "Guys, meet *mi amor*."

Velez lifts his head and groans. "Help me." He has a scabbed over E and M on his forehead.

Javier chuckles. "He likes little boys. His wife was not pleased. She paid me to do this," he explains. "And Angel? He thought he was on the right side with Mendez. Remember Mendez, *manzanita*? I gutted him last night. Angel was very wrong. The right side is the only side and that's with me. Everyone that's not with me is a dead man walking."

My blood goes cold. If Javier ever discovers who I am, he won't just let me go with a slap on the wrist. This room is a real possibility. Bile rises in my throat and I choke it down.

"You'll get used to the smell," Javier tells me as he pulls on a rubber apron. "*Hermosa*, can you bring me a razor? They're in the toolbox under the hammer."

Velez starts crying as I walk over to the toolbox. I pluck a razor out and hand it to Javier. He grabs my wrist and pulls me close. His lips press to my forehead.

"So brave," he murmurs before releasing me.

I watch with horror as Javier carves a large E and an M into Velez's chest, matching the ones on his forehead. He screams as blood runs down and puddles in his chair between his legs. Javier squats and looks at Velez's purple balls. Then, without warning, he digs the razor into the man's flesh between his balls and cuts deep.

Screams.

Horrible, horrible screams.

I'm unable to look away as Javier squeezes Velez's balls and they slide out of his body like egg yolks into a bowl. Velez vomits and then passes out. All I can do is stare in utter horror.

"That's gotta fucking hurt," he says as he stands. "You next, Angel?"

Angel sobs and shakes his head. "N-No. P-Please. I can do whatever you want. I swear to you, I pledge my loyalty. I swear it, *jefe*."

Javier laughs. "*Jefe*, huh?" He walks over to Angel and pats his naked stomach, leaving Velez's blood smeared on him. "We'll see."

I expect him to hurt him too, but instead he walks over to the sink and washes up. Once he's clean and he's put the apron away, he starts whistling. He grabs my hand and pulls me out of the room.

I guess we're done.

Fuck.

He can never ever know who I am.

Ever.

It's time to step up my game because I won't end up in that room like one of those guys.

"You bought me too much," I complain.

He laughs as he drives to one of the resorts on the beach where he's made lunch reservations. "Not enough."

I shake my head at him. My necklace has a giant teardrop diamond and I also have a matching diamond tennis bracelet. I'd balked that he spent nearly 1.4 million Mexican pesos as if it were nothing. And that was just on two pieces of jewelry. He bought me dozens of outfits, a bunch of fancy shoes, and several swimsuits. I know I'm doing a job but damn, sometimes I feel like a queen with this man.

"They have the best lobster frittata," he tells me as we pull up to the valet.

Lobster frittata. Makes me think of how that man's balls were squeezed from their sac. I choke down bile. I will not be having the lobster frittata.

"Sr. Estrada," the man greets when Javier opens his door.

Javier hands him the keys before rounding the car to meet me on my side where another man opens the door for me. My hand slips into Javier's strong one. It's hard to believe this same hand brutalized a man earlier.

It's a testament to Javier's villainous character.

One minute he's torturing a man. The next, he's buying jewelry for his flavor of the week. If I were a profiler instead of a field agent, I'd assume he's a legit psychopath.

"You are the most beautiful thing this restaurant has ever seen," he croons against my hair as his arm wraps around my waist.

I melt against him, intoxicated by his words. If I'm easily charmed by a psychopath, what does that make me?

Brainless.

Stupid.

Walking a dangerous line.

His palm slides to my ass and he gives me a little squeeze. It's enough to pull me out of my head and throw me into the moment. With him. With Javier Estrada, the man who commands the attention and obedience of everyone in the room. A man in a suit greets us and I learn he's the hotel manager. He guides us into a bustling restaurant but takes us through some side doors to a lone table on a small balcony. It faces the ocean and the breeze is warm. The afternoon sun is setting. It's all so romantic.

Psychopath.

Remember, Rosa.

"Bring us something to drink," Javier orders.

The man nods and hurries off. Javier doesn't set his gun down on the table to remind people he's the badass of this city. It simply exudes from him in his confident smirk.

"Something's bothering you," he muses aloud, his sharp gaze penetrating me.

I twist the new bracelet around my wrist and shrug. "Some things you just can't unsee."

His warm hand covers both of mine. *"Lo siento,* Rosa." *I'm sorry, Rosa.* "That was too gruesome for you to witness." His black brows are furled together in a concerned way. It makes my heart rate pick up.

"I know you're a baddie," I say, hoping to lighten the mood. "Sometimes I forget the level, though. You're good to me and that's all that matters."

"He was good to me, mija. I fell for a bad man because he was good to me."

My mother's words ring loud and clear in my head. She was desperately in love with one of El Paso's worst gangsters. He killed and thieved and tortured. My own flesh and bone was a villain and my mother loved him. The irony is not lost on me.

"That is all that matters," he agrees. "When I claim something as my own, I treat it well. Do my men look like they hurt for anything?"

"They all have cars that cost more than most people's homes," I say with a snort.

He grins wide, his dimple forming. "Their bank accounts are even bigger. When something is mine and they pledge one hundred percent loyalty to me, they are rewarded." His thumb brushes along my bracelet. "You are being rewarded."

I drag my stare from his piercing one and stare off into the ocean. "Have any of them betrayed you?" I can't look at him because he might see I'm betraying him too.

His fingers link with my left hand. "None who have ever lived to tell about it."

Our eyes lock again and I see fire brimming in his stare. Challenging. Questioning. I should back off, but I'm clearly a masochist in wanting to know my fate because I continue.

"Girlfriends? I never see you with anyone. Sure, I've seen you with women, but they never stay. Not after a little fun. Why's that?" There are some questions that need answering and it has nothing to do with the agency.

"I haven't found one worth keeping." His answer is simple and it makes my heart swell.

God, I'm so deeply fucked with this man.

"And I'm worth it?" I bite on my lip, ignoring the way butterflies dance in my belly.

"You are to me." He tugs my hand so I'm stretched forward over the table. His lips press to the back of my hand that's locked in his. "Completely worth it. You're a mysterious package I'm enjoying opening layer by layer. When I get to the center, I know you'll be completely mine."

"What if you don't like what you find?" I ask, my voice catching and tears threatening. I'm getting swept up in the storm that's Javier Estrada. Desperate to be in the center where it's calm. I want to cling to him and forget everything around us. That would make life much simpler. This having to be two people is tricky. A part of me likes the woman I am when I'm in his arms. Sexy, beautiful, fierce, and strong. When I'm Rosa Daza, CIA agent, and with Michael, I feel dirty and tired and overworked. I'm not the confident woman I am now. It confuses me because I'm not supposed to be a better person with a wanted man. Everything is supposed to be worse, not better.

"I'm pretty sure I like everything about you, *manzanita*. Even the parts you hold dear to your heart." He lets out a heavy sigh. "And it doesn't matter if I don't like what I find. You're already mine."

I want to discuss this more—to probe him on what he'll do if he ever finds out—but the man is back with a bottle of Armand de Brignac Brut Gold Champagne. He pops the cork and pours the bubbly alcohol into our champagne flutes. I'm in a daze as he rattles off the specials. Javier, sensing I can't decide, chooses for us both and waves the man away.

"Rosa," he murmurs, his voice harsh despite how quiet he is. "A toast." He holds up his glass and indicates I should do the same.

I grab my crystal flute that's filled nearly to the brim and hold it up. His hand has never let go of mine and I can't help but cling on to the fact he won't hurt me if he ever discovers the truth. "A toast to what?"

"A toast to what is happening between us. My father told me stories of my mother. How when he saw her, he knew she was his. Pursued her relentlessly. Fucked a child into her and married her not long after. He said *Mamá* was like the sun. Brilliant and hot and dangerous to a man like him. But he wanted her to burn him anyway." His eyes darken and I try not to melt under his heated gaze. "I have no doubts you will burn me, *manzanita*. I can feel it just below the surface. Like an alligator beneath the water, just ready to strike. It's going to hurt. It's going to hurt so fucking bad and yet…"

Tears prickle my eyes and my bottom lip trembles. "And yet we want it anyway."

He nods and tilts his head. "Here's to sweet motherfucking pain. It is our future."

We both suck down our champagne, the air charged with many emotions. Anger. Lust. Need. Desperation.

I'm not rattled and upset like I should be because he knows this can't end well and is still here. He feels it down to his bones and yet he's here with me anyway.

I'm worth it to him.

A sob catches in my throat that has him rising from his chair. He rounds the table and pulls me into his arms. His warm strength envelops me and I allow myself to fall. Just for a moment. I get sucked up into him and I seek out the eye of the storm. It's safe there. Nobody gets struck with flying debris. It's warm and sunny and ours.

"*Música, por favor,*" he barks out to someone.

Seconds later, a romantic Mexican song fills the air. He pulls my arms up and I lock my fingers behind his neck. His palms fall to my waist as he rocks with me slowly. I can't look at him. He'll see the secrets I harbor. That I'm supposed to be taking him down and all I want to do is fall deeper into this thing we're doing. To pretend I am his Rosa Delgado…forever.

Rosa Daza has been snuffed out for four years.

Does she even exist anymore?

I tilt my chin up, hot tears welling in my eyes. "We need to use protection. I need the morning after pill. We're being careless." I'm telling him without telling him we can't be like my parents. It ends badly. We will end badly.

"Shhh," he croons, his lips brushing against mine. "You're mine, Rosa. How many times do I have to tell you this? Mine. Even if you betray me and destroy me in the process, you are mine."

"But…" I whisper.

"But nothing. This is the Estrada way. When we

know, we know."

I meet his intense stare as tears roll down my cheeks. "For the record, I want you to know, *I* want this." The real me, whoever she is now. She wants Javier Estrada and wants to forget anything else.

He doesn't let me speak anymore. Just kisses me.

The sunset our backdrop.

The sweet music our soundtrack.

Our future the credits that will roll at the end of our eventual unhappy ending.

Capítulo Doce

Javier

"He fucking stinks, *jefe*," Alejandro complains. "Can I just cut his throat and get rid of the body?"

Smirking, I shake my head. "Nope. He lives. Velez will stay alive as long as we can prolong it. Did you repack him with ice?"

"Yeah, but he's looking a little green. I don't think he's going to live much longer," he admits. "When will Yoet arrive?"

I check my watch as I stand from my desk chair. "My father and Tania are supposed to already be here. Everything is ready for the party tonight?"

It's been several days since I took Rosa shopping. That night, when I pulled her into my arms and danced with her at the hotel, she's seemed to shed some of her tension. Allowed me to fully pull her into my world. She didn't balk when I had Arturo pack up her things and bring them to my bedroom. She didn't argue when I told her she was no longer a maid. She just went with it. For this, I'm glad. She needs to realize she's mine. Now and forever.

Alejandro walks over to the window and points. "The food is prepared and guests are arriving. Rosa is ordering around the hired wait staff for the event. Is that okay, *jefe?*"

Chuckling, I walk over to where he points and watch her from the window. Despite being told she's not a maid anymore, she still oversees the maids as though it's her duty, and now the hired wait staff. She's gesturing to a table and the man she's talking to has his head bowed in submission.

My queen is on fire today.

She knows how important it is to me to impress my father and she's going out of her way to please me. If my father wasn't arriving any moment, I'd toss her over my shoulder and fuck her real good for being such an accommodating woman.

"Are they bringing their nanny?" Alejandro asks.

I'm not a fan of Camila, but she loves Emiliano as though he's her own, so I forgive her. I'm not blind to the disdainful way she regards Tania behind her back. Camila worships my father and is a beautiful woman, but Tania is his wife. She can do no wrong in my father's eyes. I believe this drives their nanny crazy. I'm sure she'd prefer if she got to play mommy along with my father.

"Camila will be here. Don't fuck her," I warn.

He chuckles. Alejandro may be a young man, but he always has eyes for the older women. The last thing I need is one of my bodyguards fucking my father's nanny. What a shitfest that would be. "I'll stay away, but you know my dick brings all the honeys to the yard."

"You won't have a dick if you disobey me," I snap back.

He's not worried by my warnings based on the smirk he still wears, but he tells me what I want to hear anyway. "I like my dick. I won't fuck the nanny."

"Good, let's go—" I start but then a shrill shriek echoes from down the hallway.

Emiliano.

I stalk out of the office in time to see a three-year-old boy with black hair clumsily running for my office. When he sees me, he holds his arms out. I eat up the distance and scoop my baby brother into my arms.

"Emi," I coo as I kiss the top of his head. "I missed you, *hermanito." Little brother.*

"Javi! Pool!" he says, his pudgy fingers tugging at the knot on my tie.

I chuckle as I walk down the hallway with Alejandro on my heels. In the foyer, my father and his wife, Tania, stand looking weary from their travels. Father wears a three-piece suit and tie, which makes me glad I decided to wear one as well. He's fussing over Tania as she tries to untangle her sunglasses from her long, inky black hair. My father is of my size and build, but he's gone fully gray. His skin is tanner than mine as he spends a good portion of his time on the beach and by the pool. At fifty-two, he's still a good-looking man. Always smiling and charismatic. It's no wonder how he was able to rope such a hot looking wife.

"Javier," Tania greets, her pouty lips forming a smile upon seeing me. "Come here, love."

Emiliano wiggles out of my arms and takes off sprinting to explore more of the house. Camila, wearing her usual sour expression, chases after him. Tania pulls me into a hug, her fat fake tits smashed against my chest.

She smells like one of the new perfumes I bought Rosa.

"How are you?" I ask.

She pulls away and smiles, her fake lashes batting against her cheeks. "Perfect as always. How is my favorite stepson?"

Father chuckles from behind her as he possessively pulls her back into his arms. I am of no threat to him with Tania, but she's closer to my age than his. He doesn't let her get far from him. Ever. She seems to prefer it that way as she melds against him.

"All is well in Acapulco," I tell her with a grin.

Father kisses her head and then releases her to hug me. "I've missed you, *mijo*."

I pat his back and then gesture to the open doors overlooking the backyard and ocean. "You must put your things away and relax after your travels. Everything is ready for your arrival."

Father flashes me a grin of approval. "We'll change into our suits. I look forward to catching up."

Tania clutches onto his elbow and Alejandro shows them to where they'll be staying. It's where they always stay. Father's bodyguards follow after them. I take the moment to seek out Rosa. She's still outside and is fussing over a flower arrangement over one of the tables. I sneak up behind her and wrap my arms around her.

"Time to party, *mami*," I growl against her ear.

Her pink summer dress is thin and I love how it hugs her curvy body, but I want to see her in a swimsuit more.

"Change into your swimsuit. Party is getting started and I want you to officially meet my father," I say, my hands sliding up to her fat tits.

She turns in my arms, a frown on her pretty face.

"What if he doesn't like me?"

I chuckle. "You are beautiful. Father loves pretty things. Go change."

"I hope you're right."

"I'm always right."

It's taken her much longer than I expected for her to change. I already swapped out my suit for black swim trunks. Tania and Father have long since come to the pool. What's taking so fucking long?

"I heard about the Osos," Father says as he sips from a mini bottle of tequila. He prefers them over glasses. The same sized ones they stock hotels and airplanes with. I make sure to have plenty to keep Father happy. And as his son, I drink them too when he's around.

"The Osos no longer exist." I down the small bottle and deposit it on the side of the pool. Despite the cool breeze, the water is heated to perfection.

"Who are our threats now?" Father asks.

I shrug and then rest my arms on the edge of the pool as I stare at the ocean. "Arturo is analyzing our next moves. Everything is in chaos. Mayor is missing. Police are wisely protecting their only money-making assets left, the local hotels along the beach. The city is nothing but bloodshed and horror."

Father chuckles. His back is against the pool side as he watches Tania play with Emiliano in the shallow end. "Business is up in Puerto Vallarta. New hotels being built all the time. The Estradas own most of the expansion. It's how I was able to buy my new yacht."

I narrow my eyes and focus on the massive beast out beyond the waves. "That's yours?"

"It is. She cuts through the water as though she's Moses parting the Red Sea. The waters yield to her command."

"It's safe for Emi?"

"Of course it is. There's no way he could accidentally fall off. When on the yacht, not only does Camila watch after him, but I've assigned my two most trusted men to also watch. He's precocious but intelligent. Your brother has a healthy respect for the ocean. Unlike someone I know," he teases.

I chuckle. "Cliff diving has nothing to do with respect for the ocean. It's about knowing your abilities. I'm confident in my ability of finding the deepest part to dive into. I am not careless, *Padre*."

"Of course not—holy shit," he hisses. "Look at that woman, Javi. *Ella es hermosa.*" She's beautiful.

When I turn, I grin upon seeing her. My Rosa. And she's more than beautiful. She's utterly breathtaking. She wears a two-piece white bikini that barely covers parts of her that taste like heaven. The triangles covering her nipples are tiny and the globes of her breasts are on full display for everyone, including my father. The tiny scrap that covers her bottom half is just that. A scrap. I know she's shaved smooth beneath, but I can see the dark line of her slit of her pussy lips. It will be only more transparent once she hits the water. I knew when I chose this one for her, it would be perfect. Her long dark hair is in messy waves behind her and she wears a pair of white strappy heels that make her calves more toned looking than before.

"¡Hola, mami!" I call out, pride in my voice.

She seeks me out and flashes me a brilliant smile. Her makeup is flawless. Long dark lashes. Smoky eyeshadow. Full red lips. The jewelry I've given her glimmers in the late afternoon sun, making her fucking sparkle.

"*Hola*, Javi," she greets, her voice husky and shy.

"This is your girlfriend?" Father asks, his eyes tracking her as she walks around the pool.

"*Sí*. She's perfect, yes?"

"I can certainly see why you're so taken with her," he agrees. "Let's meet the darling."

I climb out of the pool and stalk over to her, dripping wet. She lets out a squeal of surprise when I grab her and pull her against me. Her ass is bare and I'm pleased that she's wearing this thong swimsuit. It's daring but my *manzanita* is brave. My palms grip her naked ass in appreciation.

"I could fuck you right now in front of everyone," I murmur against her ear. "You're so goddamned hot that everyone here wishes you belonged to them. But you are mine, Rosa."

She melts at my words. This woman is so pliable. I can ease her into anything as long as I preempt it with something lovely whispered into her ear.

"I'm yours," she agrees.

"And I'm Yoet Estrada," my father says from behind Rosa, amusement in his voice.

She pulls away and offers her dainty hand. He takes it and kisses the top but doesn't release her. Tania, used to his flirtatious nature, doesn't even bat an eye in his direction. My father is no threat of taking my woman, but it won't stop him from being ultra friendly with her.

"Rosa Delgado," she says, her voice sultry and somehow fierce all at once. Another niggle of pride dances through me. I hug her from behind, my palms roaming all over her naked flesh. I'm hard and my cock presses against her, letting her know just how she affects me.

"Rosa is a beautiful name," he says. "Come meet my wife, Tania, and our son, Emiliano."

He tugs at her hand, forcing me to release her. I watch Rosa's perfect ass jiggle as she walks with my father toward the shallow end of the pool. Tania with Emi on her hip climbs up the steps and regards Rosa with a wide smile. They shake hands and then Rosa leans forward to ruffle Emi's hair. He beams at her and reaches for her.

My chest aches at seeing her take my brother into her arms. She hugs him to her as though he's every bit as precious to her as he is me. When she turns to seek out my gaze, her eyes shine with love and adoration. I'm stunned by how gorgeous she is in this moment. It has nothing to do with her killer body and everything to do with her instant love for my brother.

Stalking over to them, I beam at her. "He's perfect, yes?"

She nods. "So cute. Oh my God. I love him."

Emi plays with her necklace and babbles about a show called *Paw Patrol*. She nods animatedly as she listens. He equally adores her. Any apprehension I had about her meeting my family is squashed in this moment.

"Camila," Tania calls out. "It's time to put Emiliano to bed."

Camila nods, never smiling, and takes Emi from Rosa's arms. It's dusk now and the party is getting underway as the band has arrived. The atmosphere quickly evolves from family swim party to adult dance party. As the music begins booming and an up and coming new Mexican band starts playing, I tug Rosa back into my arms where she belongs. I wave for a server to bring us drinks. Real ones. He offers us shots of tequila. Once we've downed a couple and the heat is sliding through our veins, I start dancing with Rosa.

Her hips move to the beat in a provocative way that has my dick aching in my trunks. I simply hold her with her back pressed to my chest, satisfied for the skin to skin connection. Besides, our dancing can't even hold a candle to Father and Tania. A crowd forms when Father starts bobbing his head to the beat. His chest is covered with tattoos that rival mine and his trunks hang low on his narrowed hips. He may be older, but Tania is lucky to have a man like him. She wears a revealing black bikini that makes her fat tits bounce when she starts dancing too. Those two are positively in sync with one another. It's mesmerizing to watch.

"Wow," Rosa marvels aloud.

I suckle on her neck and reverently palm her stomach. "They dance well."

"You think?" she says with a laugh. "They're amazing."

Tania holds her arm out, her fingers calling for my father as her hips rock to the beat. He dances toward her as though she's reeling him in. When he's close, she pretends to push him away without touching him. He acts as though he's been struck but then dances forward again, bending his knees more and more with each step until he falls at his knees in front of her. Their dance takes a provocative turn when he grips her thigh and lifts it over his shoulder. She tugs on his hair with one hand and waves her other one above her as she moves. His lips kiss her thigh and his palms grope her ass. Then, he's back on his feet, his hips rocking against hers. Their eyes are locked on one another as they both fight for lead during their dance. His palms rake over her, tugging at her swimsuit hard enough to tease the audience with more skin but never pulling it hard enough to expose her.

"Let's go to the hot tub," I murmur, eager to touch my woman without prying eyes of everyone around us. My private hot tub would be ideal, but Father will not be pleased if I leave the party. So, I head for the big one near the pool that has several people already in it.

Marco Antonio nods, fully dressed in a black suit with a tan FN SCAR in hand—a fully automatic rifle that shoots 5.56 ammo—a constant reminder that nobody gets out of fucking line or they'll be riddled with holes like the goddamned Swiss cheese on the party platters. Nobody dares start shit. Not at an Estrada party. We're heavily protected and watched over. Everyone knows this.

"Let me help you, *mami*," I croon as I kneel in front of Rosa. I grasp her ankle and place her shoe on my knee. Quickly, I unfasten the buckle and rid her of her fancy shoe. The next one gets removed. Faces I don't recognize politely nod and then exit the waters, leaving us alone.

"Your father is nice," she says, smiling. "So is his wife."

Nice.

Her embarrassment tells me she thinks he's handsome.

"I'm glad you approve of my family." I kiss the inside

of her knee before standing.

She's much shorter without her heels. So fucking cute. I grasp her hand and guide her into the hot water. We settle with her in my lap with her back against me.

"The party is just getting started," I murmur against her ear as I grip her thighs and spread her apart.

"Yeah?" she breathes.

I like her cunt open and waiting for me. But my sweet Rosa will have to wait a little while longer. So many things I want to show her.

"Arturo," I call out.

My bodyguard snaps to attention and strides over to the side of the hot tub. "Find Iker. Tell him to bring everything." He nods and leaves.

"Who's Iker?" she questions, turning her head slightly.

I kiss her supple lips. "He's the one who makes my parties fun."

"I'm already having fun," she tells me against my mouth. "I'd have more fun if you'd actually touch me." The pout in her voice has me throwing back my head in laughter.

"I will touch you plenty," I promise. "Dessert is meant for last because you appreciate it more. You've waited so long to taste it. If we skipped to dessert each time, it would no longer be as sweet, *manzanita*."

Iker saunters our way, his bag slung over his shoulder. The kid, not much older than Alejandro, is fit and tatted up everywhere. All over his chest and face. He'd look fucking fierce except he's always high as a kite and grinning like an idiot. His swim trunks hang low on his trim waist and if they fall any more, he'll show us his pierced cock. I've seen it more times than I care to when he's gotten blitzed out of his mind at my parties.

"*Señor*," he greets as he sits down on the edge of the hot tub, his long legs dangling in the water. His eyes slide over to Rosa and they glimmer with appreciation. "I have the best shit in Guerrero tonight," he boasts. "For the beautiful lady, she will have a night she'll never forget."

I arch a brow at him. "Just the lady?"

He chuckles. "I suppose you can partake, you dirty bastard."

Most men would get shot in the face for being disrespectful, but Iker is just a little shit. You either love him or hate him. Lucky for him, I love him. I love what he offers even more. He digs around in his bag until he finds a baggie filled with pink pills. Once he has some in his hand, he slides into the water and makes his way over to us.

"Open," he instructs to Rosa.

She turns and her eyes blaze with worry. I kiss her nose and then open my mouth. Iker places a pill on my tongue and I swallow it dry.

"It's okay," I assure her.

Tentatively, she opens her mouth. Iker's eyes gleam devilishly as he feeds her a pill. I'm sure he'd love to feed her his cock as well. Over my dead body.

"Heightens sensations. You'll love me when you're fucking later," he tells me as he goes back to his bag. "Until that kicks in, I have some of the finest weed this country has seen."

As he preps his pipe, Rosa turns to whisper, "I don't know if I should."

"You should. I'll keep you safe," I promise.

He slides our way, a plume of pungent smoke exhaling from him. Like the dutiful little helper he is, he holds the pipe to Rosa's lips. She's nervous but takes a hit. When she coughs it out, both Iker and I laugh. I snag it from his grip and take my own hit. It's stout, but I can tell it's really good shit.

"You're doing so well," I praise to my girl as I blow out the smoke onto her neck. Then, I nip at her flesh with my teeth. "What else you got?" I ask Iker.

"The usual. Coke. Crystal. Uppers. Downers." He beams at me. "Roofies."

Rosa stiffens in my arms.

"I don't need to roofie my girl. She spreads her legs for me whenever I ask," I boast as I once again part her thighs.

Iker's eyes are wide and focused despite probably being fucked up right now as he stares at her through the water. The blue glow of the lights illuminates her position.

"Here, *jefe*," Arturo says as he sets down one of the server trays on the ledge beside me. It's filled with shots of tequila.

"Gracias." I pluck one from the tray and hand it over to Iker. Then, I give my girl one.

Shot after shot, we drink and cut up. Iker has some shitty jokes, but they make Rosa laugh, which in turn, makes me laugh. The more we drink and smoke, the more relaxed she gets. I love when she lets loose. Whatever pill Iker fed to us is starting to take its toll. Rosa can't stop from rubbing against my dick. And when I suck on her neck, she whimpers in such a needy fucking way. A way that has even Iker forgetting who she belongs to as he inches closer and closer.

"Let's go to your room," Rosa pleads.

Iker smirks knowingly at me. "Don't mind me."

I tug at one of the strings on her bottom bikini. Then, I tug at the other. She gasps when I pull the material from her body, revealing her perfect cunt to the other man in the hot tub. I pull her thighs apart since she seems to want to close them, and reveal everything to him.

"She's perfect, yes?" I ask him.

He nods, his eyes blazing with hunger. "*Sí.*"

"She's mine," I growl.

"*Sí,*" he rasps out, his eyes never leaving her cunt. "Look but don't touch."

I slide a finger between her slit and push inside of her. A mewl escapes her. "Her cunt is the tightest one I've ever had the pleasure of feeling," I tell him. I urge another finger inside her, loving how she whimpers in response. "Any man who thinks he can sink his cock into her cunt that belongs to me will get his throat cut. Simple."

"Simple," Iker rasps. He's hard in his trunks as he fantasizes about my woman.

"I bet you wish you could fuck her," I taunt.

His eyes flash and he nods. "If she didn't belong to an Estrada, I'd fuck her so good."

Evil bastard likes to drive me mad.

"She belongs to me, which means you can watch me fuck what you'll never have," I growl. "Bring her more."

He groans but fishes through his bag for another pill. This time she doesn't argue when he places the pill on her tongue. His finger lingers and he reluctantly pulls away. I'm buzzed, but I accept another. Marco Antonio and Arturo are nearby. Plus, Father's men are always on watch.

"Javier," Rosa whines as she wiggles in my arms until she's facing me and straddles my hips. Her eyes are heavy-lidded and her pupils wide. "I need you."

Capítulo Trece

Rosa

I'm flying high. So high. But Javier has me in his solid, protective arms. I don't even care that Iker can see bare parts of me. All I care about is Javier. I want—no, I need—him inside of me. My body physically aches for this.

"Please," I beg as I shamelessly grind against his hard cock through his trunks. "Make love to me."

He chuckles, the sound deep and dark. "In front of Iker?"

"Yes," I moan. "I don't care. I just want you."

His fingers feel like silk as he tugs away the strings on my back, freeing me of my top. I slide my body against his naked chest, enjoying the way my breasts feel smashed against him.

"Iker's cock is pierced," Javier taunts. "Sure it isn't his young cock you want inside of you instead?"

"Just yours," I plead, my fingers clawing desperately at his shorts. I manage to yank them down and free him. We both groan when I sink down on his thickness.

"What if another man fucks you?" Javier demands, his fingers biting deliciously into my hips. "What happens?"

I rock up and down on him, my fingers tangling in his hair. "You'll kill him."

He grabs hold of my hair and yanks back, baring my throat to him. "I'll kill you too if I have to." His finger slides between my pussy lips and he massages my clit. "Will I have to kill you too?"

"I won't fuck another man," I vow. "I swear, Javier. Only you."

He pinches my clit and sucks on my throat hard. Stars dance around me as he owns me completely. I come with a shriek, uncaring of those around me, and groan when his heat fills me up. His kisses on my neck are possessive. He's marking me over and over again. I let him because I want everyone to see I'm his.

But your job?

In this moment, I don't fucking care.

He pulls me closer and I curl against him, seeking his comfort. His fingers lazily stroke my spine as he kisses my hair. I'm safe with him. Safe with a monster. It doesn't make sense.

I drift off but wake to discover we're moving. I'm wrapped in a towel as Javier walks us through his cold house. He's gentle with me as he dries me off once in his room and helps me into bed. And I fall asleep with my monster bucking inside of me, owning me even as I chase sleep.

He's completely taken over.

And I'm not sure I'm even unhappy about that.

I've never felt so alive.

I'm an idiot.

Oh my God.

I fucked Javier in front of everyone at the party last night. Got high. Took drugs. Did everything the CIA would shit over if they found out. Then, like every night, I let Javier come inside me. So many times. I'm so deeply fucked I don't even know what to do anymore.

I need focus.

Thank goodness it's Saturday.

I can meet with Michael and stop my world from spinning. Seeing him will remind me of my job. Of my freaking duty.

I'd slipped out while Javier dined with his family. He thinks Michael is my ex but still my friend. Saturdays used to be my day off and Javier knows I promised to have dinner with Michael. I'm not sure how much longer he'll be okay with me spending Saturdays away from him to run off to see my ex, so I do what I can while I can. While he was distracted feeding Emiliano grapes, I left the estate and took off to the hotel.

My thoughts are a jumbled mess. Last night, I'd been nervous. I was meeting the big dog. Yoet Estrada. It was such a pivotal moment. I needed him to trust me as well. But then he was just an older version of Javier. Handsome and friendly. His wife was sweet and their son was adorable. It was hard defining who was the bad guy exactly. If anything, I wanted those people to like me. To think I was good enough to be at Javier's side.

Spinning and spinning.

I'm losing my mind.

Is this how my mother felt when she got wrapped up with my father? My mom was good and gentle. My father was a crazy gangster who somehow hooked my mother. I was made from love. Despite everything my father was into, he loved my mother.

My heart aches as I slip into the hotel. I go through my usual checks and find myself standing in front of the same hotel room as last time. I'm nervous. What if Michael can tell how far I've slipped in just a week's time? Swiping my palms on my light pink summer dress, I try to steady my nerves. Oddly enough, when I touch the dainty diamond bracelet Javier gave me, it calms me.

This morning, he spent the early hours lazily kissing me between my thighs. I'd come several times until I was too sensitive to take it anymore. Then, he just held me down and forced one more orgasm on me before sliding his cock into me. I'd been so dizzied and addicted to him I nearly decided to forgo coming to see Michael.

"If you don't show up, we'll assume you've been made. We'll be forced to come for you."

The very thought of agents busting into Javier's home, scaring little Emiliano, had me dragging out of bed with new resolve. The fact I was more concerned about the Estradas than my duties had me snapping out of it.

I have a job.

I need to remember that.

The door opens before I have a chance to knock and Michael stands there not wearing a shirt. My eyes, of their own accord, drag down his newly formed man-boobs and rounded stomach. He's only wearing boxers and his hair is disheveled. His breath reeks of alcohol and his eyes are bloodshot.

"You look like a fucking whore," he sneers, his eyes

raking over my breasts through my shirt. "Is his cum still running out of you?"

I gasp in shock. After a week of being Javier's queen, I'm stunned at being spoken to so rudely. "Excuse me?"

"Just get inside, Daza," he snaps.

Glowering at him, I push past him. Saying my last name where others could hear is reckless. I waltz inside and eye the space with disgust. I can't believe I was deluded into thinking we had something. Looking back, he just used me for sex. We didn't talk about anything. All I did was hang on his every word while he fucked prostitutes between our visits.

He's disgusting.

I pick up a folder from the table, but it gets torn from my grip by Michael and shoved in his messenger bag.

"Classified," he barks. He picks up a bottle of tequila and twists the cap. "What do you want?"

Letting out a sigh, I walk over to the bed and sit down on the edge. "I'm here to give you an update. Like always. It's Saturday."

"No shit?" he asks. "I thought you'd run off into the sunset with that fucker. You're clearly sleeping with him. That much was evident when I saw you with him."

"You told me to," I snap back, my fire brimming to the surface. "You said get close to him."

"You got close all right," he says as he scratches his balls through his boxers. "Does he make you squeal like a pig, Daza?"

"You're an asshole when you're drunk. I'm not putting up with this," I bite at him as I rise. "Tell Stokes I'll meet with him via video conference next week. I'll inform him of my updates."

As I walk past him, he grabs my bicep, his strong fingers bruising my flesh. "No."

"Yes," I hiss at him. "Let me go or I'll report this. I'll report all of this."

He shoves me away from him and I fall to my ass on his bed, the mattress springs squeaking in protest. "You're not reporting shit."

I start to rise again when he swings his half-full bottle of tequila at me. It makes contact with the side of my forehead with a loud thunk. I crumple to the bed, my vision blacking out. Blinking away my daze, I rub at the painful spot on my head.

"Michael," I croak out. "You hit me."

I try to sit up when his fist cracks against my jaw. I've never been so brutally hit before in my entire life. Pain so intense explodes across my face. I start to crawl away, but his fingers bite into my thigh and he drags me down the bed.

"No," I mutter out. "Stop."

Everything goes black for a moment and then I blink open my eyes again. I'm jolted awake when my panties get jerked down my thighs.

"Michael," I cry out. "Stop!"

His knee comes between my thighs and he overpowers me as he pries me apart. I can hear the sound of the foil of a condom ripping.

He's going to fuck me.

And instead of being worried, all I can think about is Javier.

"No!" I scream at the top of my lungs, clawing at the duvet. "Get away from me!"

I'm silenced when he pushes inside of me. His grip

finds my throat and he squeezes. Hot tears roll out of my eyes. This hurts. I can't move and he's fucking me like it's his God-given right to.

Javier will kill me.

He'll kill both of us.

I give up. All fight bleeds out of my body as I let Michael fuck me. It's not unlike all the other times. Same position. Same amount of feelings toward me, which are none. Dirty and disgusting. At least I can count on him being quick. And he sheathed his worthless cock.

I wait it out, tears leaking from my eyes, as I wonder how long Javier will let me live. Will he hold me one last time and tell me I'm safe? A loud, ugly sob tears from me as Michael groans. He comes hard and then he's pulling out of me.

"Fuck!" he curses. "Fuck, Rosa! Why did you fucking make me do that?"

I curl into a ball, my tears soaking the bed. My entire body shudders. "H-He'll kill us now. L-Look what you did," I accuse. "Why d-did you d-do that? Michael, why?"

"I don't know," he yells back. "I don't know." Something shatters against the glass mirror. "I'm fucking sorry, okay? I just missed you. I miss us."

Sniffling and my jaw aching, I sit up. My head hurts badly. He's standing on my panties, but I don't even care. I need to get out of here. Sliding off the bed, I stumble toward the door.

"Where are you going?" he demands, his eyes wild.

"I'm getting away from you," I shriek. "You've ruined everything. We're both as good as dead. He'll take us to the shed and gut us, Michael. You did this to us!"

"No," he bellows as he lunges for me. "He won't know because you'll keep your goddamned mouth shut and remember your duty to the motherfucking agency, Daza!"

We slam against the door and it cracks in protest. I scream, kicking at him, but he smashes me against the door with his weight. His grip on my biceps is strong, keeping me locked in place.

"I w-won't lie t-to him," I choke out. "Let me go."

"Will you listen to yourself? You've gone fucking crazy over him! You can't tell him shit, Rosa. He's a target, not your fucking boyfriend."

I squirm and spit in his face. He releases my arm to grip my jaw. I'm forced to look at the man whom I trusted for so long. He's more of a monster than Javier could ever be.

"You won't tell him," he hisses.

Bringing my knee up, I hit him hard in the balls. He starts howling and releases me. I rake my nails across his face before twisting the knob and running out the door. He starts after me, but once I exit the side door of the building, I realize he's not following me.

It's dark and people loiter about, but I'm not afraid.

I have to get to Javier.

I have to make him understand I didn't want it.

When I promised I wouldn't fuck another man, I meant that with every part of my being. Michael may think I'm brainwashed, but I'm not. I may have my duties for the agency, but my body made promises to a man that had nothing to do with anyone else.

Someone catcalls me from a bench, but I ignore

them, my feet pounding faster in my sandals. Everything hurts. I just want to find Javier, crawl into his arms, and let him hold me. That's all I care about right now. I'm almost to the gate when I slam into a man made of solid muscle.

I start screaming and flailing, but he's too strong for me.

"Calm down," he hisses. "It's me."

Jerking my head up, I lock eyes with Marco Antonio. His irritated stare is gone. He regards me with a mixture of fury and concern.

"I need Javier," I cry out, falling against him.

He scoops me into his arms and walks through the gate. I curl against him, praying he'll save me from certain death. It's an odd feeling being afraid of the one who will no doubt kill you yet craving his comfort at the same time.

The lights inside the house are bright as Marco Antonio carries me in. Upon entering the living room, I get a whiff of strong cigar smoke along with Javier's and Yoet's laughter.

"What the fuck?" Javier bellows. A chair scrapes across the floors and then I'm being pulled into his strong, warm embrace.

I scramble to wrap my arms around his neck. My tears that had been falling freely get caught in my throat as I start crying hysterically. Javier's heartbeat in his chest thunders against me.

"Rosa, what happened?" he demands. He's barking out orders to his men and it's all a blur to me. All I care about is him. When he tries to pull me away so he can look at me, I shriek and claw at his neck.

Yoet starts growling at his men and I hear him tell Javier to deal with me. That he'll take care of it. I cling to Javier. Deal with me how? Take me out back and put a bullet in my skull?

But we don't go outside.

When I peek out past his neck, I realize we're in his bathroom. He walks into the shower, turns it on, and then steps back out.

"*Manzanita*, listen to me," he says softly. "I cannot help you unless you talk to me."

Help me?

He eases me to my feet but doesn't let go. I'm shaking violently and weak. I grasp onto his suit lapels for dear life. Finally, I work up the courage to look at him.

His perfect, handsome face cracks open something deep within me. I want to lock him up in this moment where he thinks I'm beautiful and wonderful. Not in another moment where I admit to him that another man fucked me. He blurs as more tears form.

"Talk to me," he begs, his voice cracking. "Please."

"I d-don't w-want to d-die. I w-want t-to stay w-with you," I chatter, snot and tears running past my lips.

With his thumb, he swipes away the wetness draining from my nose and kisses my forehead. "Michael hurt you."

I cough, my sobs making me gasp for air, and buckle in his arms. He steadies me before tilting my chin back up with his knuckles.

"Yes or no, Rosa?"

"Y-Yes."

His thumb strokes my sore jaw as his eyes skim over my face. "He hit you."

I nod, my chin wobbling wildly. "D-Don't kill m-me, Javier."

Our eyes meet and hate blazes in his gaze. He knows. I don't have to tell him because he's clever and figured it out. But I tell him anyway.

"He f-forced me. I didn't want to," I whisper and then close my eyes, waiting for the worst. "I didn't w-want to."

"Oh, Rosa," he growls.

I wince as I wait for it to come. The wrath. The fury. A knife. A bullet. His fist. But instead of the worst, he pulls me to him. He strokes my back and hisses violent whispers speaking of revenge and murder.

Not mine.

Michael's.

And he's sorry?

"I will skin that motherfucker alive," he vows. "I didn't realize you were going, *mi amor*. I'm so sorry. *Lo siento mucho*."

I jerk my head up and our eyes lock. Tenderness and sadness are in his dark brown gaze. "You're not going to kill me?"

"No, Rosa. I'm going to clean you."

Capítulo Catorce

Javier

Red.

Red.

Fucking red.

I've never seen a woman so broken in my entire life. So fucking terrified. And she's not just any woman. She's my woman. My brave, intelligent, sexy Rosa.

That asshole raped her.

Stuck his worthless dick inside of something that belongs to Javier Motherfucking Estrada. He just made the biggest mistake of his goddamned life. I will hunt that man down and the things I've done to Velez or Mendez will seem like child's play compared to what I'll do to Michael.

He broke her.

He broke my sweet Rosa.

I've managed to undress us both and have pulled her under the hot stream of the shower. Still, she clings to me. Desperately so. If I had any fears or suspicions about her, they've been squashed for the time being. She needs me. Rosa Delgado, my maid turned lover, needs my protection.

"What hurts?" I ask as I run the bar of soap over her body.

"Everything," she whimpers. Her tears have slowed now that she realizes I'm not going to kill her. I don't know where she got the idea I would take her life over something she had no control over. If anything, it's a testament to her loyalty to me.

"What hurts the worst? Your pussy?" I set the soap down and rinse us both off.

She shakes her head. "No, that's okay. My face hurts where he punched me, though." Her fingers brush along her temple. "And where he hit me with the tequila bottle."

My blood boils, but I refrain from raging and destroying my entire goddamned house. Instead, I pepper kisses on her sad face.

"A man should not hit a woman. Ever." My words are icy and hate-filled. "He will pay."

Her brows scrunch together, but she nods. Whatever friendship she thought she would continue to carry on with him bleeds from her and gets sucked down into the drain at our feet.

"I feel so dirty," she whispers. "I don't like that he was inside me."

I can tell where she's going with this and I don't know what to fucking do. I don't like the idea of him inside of her either.

"Javier…" she trails off.

I grit my teeth and nod. "I'll make him go away."

She clutches onto my shoulders as I grip her ass. I lift her and her legs wrap around my waist. My mouth presses to her swollen lips and I kiss her gently. She reaches between us, guiding my cock inside of her. A sob catches in her throat, causing me to pull away.

"Rosa…"

"Don't stop," she begs tearfully. "Please."

I kiss her in a way that promises no one will ever hurt her again. My hips slowly thrust against her. I don't want to hurt her. I just want to help her not feel so dirty. She doesn't come, not that I expect her to.

We kiss until my balls seize up. It satisfies me as my cock spurts out my seed, marking her once again as mine. Michael is nothing more than a bad memory to us.

But for him?

His motherfucking nightmare is just beginning.

I will spend every second of every day hunting his ass down.

"Thank you," she murmurs, her body trembling.

"You're mine. Don't ever forget, *manzanita*."

I shove my Desert Eagle into my holster that's strapped to my chest and pull on a jacket over it. I'm wearing dark jeans and my steel-toed boots. My body thrums with fury.

Michael.

He's going to die by my hand.

"Does the last name check out?" I ask Arturo as we storm out to Alejandro's Hummer.

"No, *jefe*. It's a fake. Marco Antonio searched the room Michael *Brown* stayed in, but he'd already vacated the premises by the time he got there." He holds his fist out to me. "He found these."

At seeing Rosa's panties in his grip, a growl rumbles in my chest. I snatch them from his hand and shove them in my pocket. "I want you to find out everything you can about him."

"And Rosa?" he asks.

I climb into the Hummer and fire up the engine. "I want Michael."

"*Sí*," he answers as he hops in beside me.

Alejandro rode with my father and Marco Antonio to the hotel but turned up nothing. They've headed north into the city to expand their hunt. I've left Rosa in Tania's hands. My stepmother may be a party girl, but she's maternal in nature and was horrified to learn of what happened to Rosa. With my father's men still at the estate, I feel as though I've left her in good hands.

"I want to go to the hotel," I tell him and point in the direction. "Keep your eyes peeled for a fat fuck, white-ass American prowling the streets. I want you to get the word out. There's a hefty reward for whoever brings him to me alive. Five million pesos."

He leans back in his seat and starts texting. Arturo has many contacts all over Mexico and in the United States. I have no doubts in his abilities to dig up information on anyone.

Anyone.

Everyone.

He will find me Michael no matter the cost.

That motherfucking pig will pay and soon.

When we arrive at the hotel, people loiter outside, but once they see me climb out, they run. I pull my Desert Eagle from my holster and stalk into the building. There's no front desk person when we arrive. Marco Antonio already told me he found the room, so we head straight for it.

Arturo is at my back as we rush down the putrid hallway to the only rented room in the building. I kick the door open, cracking it off its hinges, and stalk inside. It appears as though it's been hastily packed and vacated. The used condom on the floor near the bed has my blood boiling again. We ransack the place looking for clues, even though I know Marco Antonio did a thorough job, as to where Michael went. When we turn up nothing, I pull a pack of matches from my pocket.

"He won't be coming back," I tell Arturo as I pluck out a match and swipe it along the back of the pack to ignite it. Once I toss it on the bed, I wait to make sure it catches fire. As soon as it alights, it moves quickly across the cheap fabric. "Let's go."

We exit the room and push through the doors where the Hummer waits. It won't be long before this shitty-ass hotel burns to the ground. All memories of where that fat fuck raped Rosa will be incinerated.

He's next.

I climb into the Hummer and turn the engine over. I barely wait for Arturo to get in before I'm peeling out, headed for the shed. Michael's not there obviously, but I have a plan. Rage blazes within me. I wish I could go back home and hold my sweet Rosa, but vengeance is what fuels me.

Nobody touches what's fucking mine and lives to tell about it.

We pull up to the shed and I rush inside, eager to fuck someone up. If Velez is still breathing, he won't be for much longer. I can hear the kid hollering, but Velez is quiet. When I burst through the doors, my lip curls up in disgust.

"Fuck, it stinks in here," I grumble.

"He's dead," Angel moans. "He's rotting and I can't feel my leg." He's no longer hanging by the ceiling but is chained by his ankle to a bolt in the floor. Vomit is on the floor around him. I'd fucking puke too if I had to smell this shit all day.

"Cut him loose, Arturo," I bark and motion for Angel.

"W-What? You're letting me go?" Angel chokes out.

"You want to be El Malo so bad," I say as I approach Velez. "Now's your chance to prove yourself."

"I won't let you d-down, *jefe*," he vows, his teeth chattering with adrenaline.

"I know," I tell him simply. "If you do, I'll squeeze your nuts from your body like Velez here, but I'll make you eat them."

He gags and I laugh. Squatting, I inspect Velez. His arm is stretched in the air, purple and ugly looking. The rope tied around his cock is doing its job. His puny pecker is stretched beyond what looks humanly possible and is the same color as his arm. Green puss bleeds from his piss hole. Soft, raspy breathing is coming from him, but he's out of it. Time to wake up. I stand and stalk over to where my apron hangs. I pull it over my head and find my hammer. By the time I turn around, Arturo is watching me with an expectant gleam in his eyes. Angel is shivering, but his stare is glued on me.

"Velez," I bark as I tap the blunt end of the hammer on the top of his skull.

He groans and lifts his head. Drool hangs from his mouth and his eyes are bloodshot. "Uhnnn."

I bend over so I can look straight into his dead eyes. "If an American was seeking safety in Guerrero, where would he go?"

His eyes roll back in his head and it lolls to the side. Not good enough. I step back and swing the hammer hard across the side of his knee. The crack is loud, but his scream is louder. I smirk, knowing I just broke his kneecap.

"If an American was seeking safety in Guerrero, where would he go?"

"I-I don't know—"

Whack!

This time, I hit his other knee. He vomits and it sprays me. Thank fuck I'm wearing my apron. I nudge the ice pack between his thighs, hoping to inflict some pain. He groans some, but when I tap his stretched out cock with the hammer in a threatening way, he starts sobbing like a little bitch.

"I-I t-think attorney g-general Lucas Lorenzo." He hisses in pain. "Please kill me."

"Tell me what I want to know and I will," I seethe.

He nods quickly. "Uh, Lorenzo lives n-north of t-the city. If t-there was an American seeking shelter, he'd w-want that f-for his p-political g-gain."

Turning to Arturo and Angel, I point at the kid. "Get him some clothes. His task is to bring me Michael. Alive. I want him sitting in this chair."

"I will find him," Angel vows.

"And me?" Arturo asks. "What will I do?"

I stand and eye Velez's stinking body. Without warning, I swing the clawed end of the hammer against the side of his skull. It lodges itself in his head, killing him on impact. "Take care of the fucking corpse."

Capítulo Quince

Rosa

One week later...

"**J**efe wanted me to ask if you wanted something to drink."

I jump at his sudden appearance and regard Angel with a forced smile. "I'm fine. Thank you."

The kid somehow narrowly escaped death at the shed. Whatever Javier did to him has him loyal as can be. He's fierce and dedicated to his new boss. When he's not at the estate, he's exhausting every minute "hunting down a pig." I can only take it to mean they're still searching for Michael.

Michael Brown.

Not Stiner.

I lied to Javier. I had to. I couldn't tell him he needed to be looking for special agent Michael Stiner with the United States Central Intelligence Agency. There's no telling what he'd do to me. I sure as hell will do whatever it takes to make sure I don't find out.

"Where did you meet him?"

"At a restaurant in Acapulco."

"What is he doing here in Guerrero?"

"He's a journalist studying the exponential increase of police corruption since the '50s."

"How long were you two seeing each other?

"Five and a half years."

"Long before you came to work for me?"

"Yes."

"Kind of random two Americans meet in my city, no?"

"It's a small world."

"El Paso, Texas, huh?"

"Born and raised."

Somehow, I gave him morsels of the truth without
giving him much to go on. Michael and I met at Langley
in Virginia. Five and a half years ago. We started sleeping
together right away. Some truth mixed into lies.

"Jefe insists." The kid, I learned, is almost twenty.
He's tall and lanky. His cheeks are still hollowed out and
his skin pale from his stint in the shed.

I rise from the couch in the living room and start for
the kitchen. It's pouring down rain today. The house feels
emptier than usual. Yoet and his family left for home a
couple of days ago and the maids are out enjoying their
day off. It's just me and Angel and Marco Antonio. Javier
and the others are out.

For a solid week now, Javier has been positively obsessed with locating Michael.

What happens when he finds him?

Will Michael rat me out?

He won't. I know Michael. He's lost himself over the
years, but his heart was always with the agency. That's
one reason why he couldn't ever buckle down and com-
mit to me. It was always about the job. Our mark. We

were trained in the event we were ever tortured for information. You don't give up information to save yourself.

But I'm not sure the CIA even had the brainpower to dream up all the ways Javier can torture a man.

I shudder as I hunt down a bottle of tequila in the kitchen. I'm tired of feeling on edge worrying if tonight will be the night Javier finds out about who I am. I've pushed him away. We fucked the night Michael raped me, but we haven't touched since. Each night, I curl up in his bed with my back to him. He doesn't come home until late and he gets up before dawn. A few times, I've found his strong arm wrapped around me in the middle of the night, but it's a reminder of how he can crush me.

He will crush me.

At some point.

I can feel it buzzing in my veins as though it's a living, breathing entity. I can't eat. I can't sleep. I've chewed my once long nails down to tiny, bloody nubs. He says I'm not to clean the house, but I sometimes find myself going behind the other maids and dusting or mopping just to clear my head.

"Javier said no liquor," Angel says from behind me.

I turn to face him and unscrew the lid. "Are you going to take it from me?"

His jaw clenches. "I don't know."

"You won't because if you touch me, Javier will feed you your own teeth," I snap.

"Miss Rosa," he groans. "Please."

Shrugging, I tilt the bottle and take a long pull of the liquid fire. His fists clench and worry dances in his brown-eyed stare.

"Don't worry, runt," Marco Antonio mutters as he

enters the kitchen. "He knows how stubborn she is. You're off the hook. Go follow the leads you texted me about earlier. I've got this."

Angel relaxes, seemingly relieved before he bolts from the kitchen. Marco Antonio prowls closer but stops a few feet away, leaning his hip against the counter.

"Actions like that could get the kid killed," he muses aloud.

"Trying to take my tequila will get him killed," I snap back.

Marco Antonio chuckles as he holds his hands up in defense. "Noted." His eyes are penetrating as he regards me. I hate how he's always searching for answers. He's Javier's most trusted man, so he's always under the assumption I'm going to betray Javier in some way. His instincts are good. I will betray Javier. The agency is probably pulling together a task force to extract me as we speak. I learned that Javier burned down the hotel, which was our intelligence hub. Everything is falling to shit and they'll be forced to act soon. Each creak of the house or bang of a shutter from the wind has me jumping out of my skin assuming the CIA is moving in on us.

I need to speak to Stokes.

Problem is, Michael is my contact. I am only to reach out to Stokes via unsecured lines if Michael has been compromised because it's a risk to the entire operation. But I can't keep sitting around doing nothing, hoping it will all just go away. Truth be told, I'd much rather just get absorbed into Javier's world and forget I'm a CIA operative. At least Javier cares about me. It's evident in his words and actions. Hell, he's on a murderous hunt for someone who hurt me. His loyalty is fierce and unyielding.

My loyalty is nonexistent.

That's not true, though. My feelings for Javier have clouded my judgment. And with Michael doing what he did, I'm overwhelmed with confusion. Right and wrong have switched teams, leaving me spinning between them.

"You're going to get shitfaced," Marco Antonio warns, his head dipping at me.

I realize I've been chugging the bottle. My body feels warm and the edginess is beginning to bleed from me, leaving me languid and relaxed. "So?"

"You need to stop. Javier will not be pleased."

I arch a challenging brow at him, emboldened by the alcohol. "Touch me and he'll kill you," I threaten.

At this, he rolls his eyes. "I don't want you, Rosa. Javier knows this. My loyalty is with him, and by proxy, you. However, if forced to choose, I'll always choose him. He's my brother."

I know he doesn't mean his actual brother, but they're close as though they're related. Sticking my tongue at him, I make a great show of taking another long pull of the alcohol. He glowers at me.

"I'll forcibly take that from you," he warns.

"You can try," I snap.

With quick movements, he prowls my way. My movements are clumsy and sluggish, but I haven't forgotten my training. I've taken down men bigger than him. I set the bottle down and reach for something to use as a weapon. The closest thing is an apple. I lob it at him and it thunks him in the head. It only serves to anger him. He lunges at me and I dip out of his intended grip. The knife block is close. I reach for it and grab hold of the meat cleaver. I swing it around, aiming for his fat head.

His strong hand grips my wrist.

"You're a fucking psycho, Rosa!"

I kick at him and land a hard hit to the side of his knee that has him faltering in surprise, but he doesn't let go of my hand holding the knife. When I go to kick him again, he shoves me against the counter, using his weight against me. I'm no match for his two hundred plus pounds.

"Let me go!"

"No," he growls. "You're wasted because you haven't fucking eaten anything in days and you're losing your damn mind."

I squirm and scream and spit at him, but he doesn't move. His massive body crushes mine against the countertop. He gives my wrist a violent shake and the cleaver falls to the floor with a loud clatter. His foot kicks it away. Then, he twists me around. I yell at the top of my lungs when he yanks both hands behind me.

"Hold still," he barks as he twists something around my wrists.

I panic and thrash, but he's too strong. Too expert with his movements.

"A zip tie?" I screech. "You just have those handy in your pocket?"

He chuckles. "Of course I fucking do, Rosa. It's my job." With that, he twists me around and hoists me over his giant shoulder. I'm wearing a pair of cotton shorts and a thin long-sleeved shirt. I don't like that his hands are touching my thighs.

Hot tears form in my eyes as he carries me. "P-Please don't touch me."

He stiffens. "I'm not like that sick fuck who hurt you.

I'm just keeping you safe until Javier gets back."

"Bring her to my office," Javier's low, seductive voice growls from the shadows.

Terror claws its way up inside of me. I don't know why he sounds so dark and ominous, but I have a clue. He knows. He has to know. I'm going to die tonight.

I try to look for Javier but from my position, I can barely move. Tears flood down my face as I await my fate. I know when we reach Javier's office because I get a whiff of his heady scent. Bad guys smell so good.

"What happened?" Javier demands. "Put her down so I can look at her."

I'm dropped to my feet, but Marco Antonio's massive hand grips my bicep to keep me from running away. Javier's back is to me as he stares out the window, both hands on his hips. Today he's dressed in his hunt-down-Michael outfit. Dark jeans. Boots. A white tank top. His Desert Eagle sits in his holster at his side. He cracks his neck and if he wasn't so hot, he'd look positively terrifying. Broad shoulders. Ink crawling along each area of bared flesh. Muscles everywhere. Even his stance is threatening.

"She tried to hit me with a meat cleaver," Marco Antonio says, amusement in his tone.

Javier snaps to attention and jerks around. His eyes blink in confusion. "What?"

"He stole my tequila," I argue with a pout. I may be about to die, but I'm feeling quite petulant at the moment. Like a spoiled child who didn't get a second piece of chocolate cake.

"All this chaos because you were trying to get fucked up, *manzanita*?" Javier asks, a black brow arched.

God, he's so hot.

No dimple today. All of his features are sharp and focused. He's in full-on cartel badass mode. And I'm desperate to fuck him like this. I want to fuck the bad guy who'll probably kill me. Desperately so. It's a revelation I'll mull on later, but right now, I want him. In all of his nefarious glory.

The end is near, I can feel it.

"So let me get this straight," he mutters as he reaches into his pocket and pulls out his switchblade. It flips out and the metal glints under the light. Thunder cracks beyond the window, making my heart race. "You're in my house being a drama queen over a fucking drink while my men and I are out there busting our asses to find your ex-boyfriend." He approaches me and pokes the tip of his blade between my breasts. "One would assume you aren't grateful."

I don't know the answer here. Am I supposed to condone his wanting to kill a fellow agent? Agent Daza says fuck that and craves to kick him in the balls. But the raped and abused woman, Javier Estrada's girlfriend, Rosa Delgado nods. She whispers, "I'm grateful."

His features soften and the agent inside of me is once again pushed into the shadows. One day soon, I'll go into town and try to reach Stokes. Today is not that day. I'm playing games with a monster and I'm enjoying them.

He grips a fistful of my shirt and pulls it away from my body. I stare down in fascination as he cuts my shirt in two. Then, with his strong, warm fingers, he pushes the fabric over my shoulders on each side, exposing my front to him. Next, the bra gets cut between my breasts. He shoves the now empty cups to the side, revealing my tits to both him and Marco Antonio.

With a snap of his head, he glowers at Marco Antonio. "She turn you on?"

"No," Marco Antonio answers without hesitation. "She belongs to you."

Satisfied, Javier gives him a clipped nod before regarding me. "I want to punish you. For riling up my men and causing strife. Angel almost got his throat cut when I ran into him in the carport. For disobeying me, *mami*. I told him to not let you drink."

Guilt rises up inside me. Angel is only trying to do his job. It's not his fault his choices were either die brutally or work for the king of the Mexican cartel doing shit jobs like babysit his bratty girlfriend. "I'm sorry," I choke out. And I am. I feel bad that I'm letting my feelings infect everyone around me.

I'm losing touch.

This is supposed to be a job.

Yet, it's not.

I do everything now based on how it makes me feel. Javier fills a void inside of me I desperately crave. A void that's been there since the day my mother died. He's good to me. Treats me like a queen. Sometimes I wish I truly were just a maid. I wish I didn't have a duty to my country to take him down.

It would be so easy to fall.

To fall for the devil with an angel's smile.

He leans forward and kisses between my breasts, his hot breath tickling me. "Your heart is racing," he observes. "How should I punish you?"

"I-I don't know."

Marco Antonio remains quiet. A statue with a death

grip on me. I wonder if this is awkward for him. One wrong move, one stray look or touch, and he could be as good as dead. Javier is serious when it comes to me. Possessive as can be.

Warmth trickles through me.

The way he wants me so fully is addicting.

"A spanking?"

I blink at him in shock. "You're not going to kill me?"

Marco Antonio snorts and Javier smirks. "Do you have a death wish? What is it with you and thinking I always want to kill you?" He runs the tip of the blade low along my stomach. Then, he rubs it gently along my shorts over my pussy, careful to focus on where my clit is. With the material protecting me, it kind of feels good. I let out a ragged breath that has Javier grinning.

His dimple.

God, it's perfect.

"I think you get off on danger," Javier muses aloud. "The fact I'm using the same knife I cut open hundreds of men should terrify a sweet girl like you, but here you are squirming and moaning. You're soaking your little panties because you don't know if I'll be gentle or rough, but either way you're desperate for the attention. You want to trust me."

"I do," I admit, my voice breathy. "I like it."

He continues his relentless rubbing with his knife against my clit. "Like what, *manzanita*? That I can't fucking go one second without thinking about you?"

"Mmhmm," I moan. "I love that."

"You like I'm so fucking obsessed with you I've abandoned my duties to find that motherfucker to avenge you?"

"Yes," I whisper, horrified I'm telling him the truth that's inside my heart. The agency doesn't matter right now. Michael sure as hell doesn't.

"Do you want me to fuck a baby inside you and force you to wear my ring?"

My lashes flutter as I give in to the way he pleasures me. "Javier…"

"Admit it," he roars, the knife pressing into me almost painfully. "Admit you want to be mine in every sense of the word."

"I do," I murmur, tears welling in my eyes. I seek his gaze out, desperate for his heated stare on mine.

"I know you're not telling me everything about yourself," he mutters lowly, his words a violent whisper. He doesn't cease his rubbing with the knife. I'm dizzy with the need to come, but his words rattle me. "I know you have secrets. Secrets I will find out."

I bite down on my bottom lip as my tears leak out. "Javier," is all I can say. I won't lie to him, not right now in this intimate yet terrifying moment, but I also can't offer the truth.

"I'm going to have to kill you one day," he snaps angrily, but his motions still dead set on bringing me to orgasm. He leans forward and presses a kiss to the corner of my mouth. "Burned by the sun. Hurts so motherfucking much, but goddamn it's beautiful."

I cry out as my orgasm steals over me. I've barely had time to come down before he's wrenching down my shorts and panties. He closes his knife and pockets it much to my relief.

"Fear makes her wet," he tells Marco Antonio. "She can look danger in the eye and come like a bad little girl.

I don't fucking know what to do about her." He runs his fingers through his gelled hair, messing it up.

Marco Antonio, realizing Javier is a slave to his confused rage, says nothing.

"Hold her legs," Javier growls. "I need to see just how wet she is."

Wordlessly, Marco Antonio grabs me beneath the back of my legs just under my ass and lifts me. He pulls my thighs apart so I'm open and for Javier's viewing pleasure. Instead of looking, Javier turns and walks over to his desk. He reaches into his desk and produces a lighter. My heart skitters in my chest. Will he burn me? Then, he pulls out one of his candy apple little cigars.

I smile.

Javier's eyes dart to mine and he studies my face. His eyes dart all over my features as though there are answers to be found. "Your cunt is practically dripping," he growls and then stalks my way. I don't flinch because he's too beautiful. Unlike Michael, I don't fear he'll strike me. With Javier, I feel like he'll completely obliterate me. And I'm not at all opposed to seeing how that will feel.

With his little cigar, he rubs the tip against my still sensitive clit. A moan escapes me and my breasts jiggle with the movement.

Javier's dark, evil eyes penetrate mine as he begins pushing the tip of his little cigar inside of me. It's thin, smaller than his finger, but I like it. The gasps of air coming from me reveal how turned on I am. Slowly, a dimple forming on his face, he fucks me with his cigar.

"Slides in and out so easy, *manzanita*. Dirty, bad liar. Little girl who likes to start trouble. Look how your cunt loves danger." He flips the top on his lighter and a flame pops up. I don't even worry that he'll burn me with it. I'm more worried about catching fire with the way he touches me with his cigar.

He slides the cigar from my pussy and holds it up, inspecting it. "So wet. You've nearly ruined my cigar," he murmurs. Then he inhales it. "Candy apples. Sweet. So fucking sweet." With eyes searing into mine, he places the little cigar between his full lips and lights the end. It has trouble lighting and his cheeks suck in hard, trying to help it along. Eventually, the end burns cherry red. Evil delight dances in his eyes as he pockets the lighter. He pulls the cigar away and grins, flashing me his perfect dimple before he curves his mouth into an "O" and blows the smoke out.

I'm intoxicated by him.

Forget the alcohol.

I'm drunk off Javier Estrada.

The bad guy I'm hot over.

He takes another puff of his cigar and then leans into me. I open my mouth, accepting him. With a pleased look on his face, he blows the smoke into my mouth. His finger touches my soaked flesh and he slides a finger inside me. "Danger makes you come. It's as though we were made for each other. The angel who only gets wet for the devil." He curls his finger inside of me, seeking out my G-spot. I'm so lost to him. All I can do is surrender to the way he plays my body. "You're nothing but a good girl who likes to be bad."

I squirm, eager for another orgasm, but Marco Antonio keeps me locked in his grip. Javier lazily fingerfucks me as he devours me with his gaze. He takes his time with both me and his cigar, clearly enjoying every moment.

"Your lips make me lose my goddamn mind," he snarls as though he's angry. I cry out when he leans forward and grabs my bottom one between his teeth. He pulls away, almost to the point of pain, with my lip locked between his teeth. The pain and fear mixed with the way he touches me has me seeing stars. I throw my head back, despite the way he bites me, when my orgasm slices through me. His teeth cut through my flesh at my action, a sharp, burning pain darting across my lip as metallic blood floods my mouth.

I don't care.

I'm so far gone, I can't find my way back.

He growls and curses at me once he realizes I'm bleeding. "You did that on purpose," he accuses, fire dancing in his eyes. The blood on his teeth has me aching for him to bite me everywhere.

"Javier," I plead. "I need to touch you."

His eyes narrow. "I haven't even punished you yet. Your punishments keep adding up, *manzanita*, long before you can ever fulfill them."

"Please…"

"Put her on her knees and then go," he barks at Marco Antonio. "She can suck my dick until I'm satisfied she's a thankful woman for all I've done to keep her safe."

Marco Antonio agrees with a grunt and then carefully sets me down on the hard floors. My wrists remain bound at my back and my lip hurts, but I'm desperate to touch Javier. I stare up at him, waiting for him to give me his cock.

"Fuck," he groans. "You're so beautiful it's maddening." He drops his cigar to the floor and stubs it out with his boot, uncaring that he may ruin the floor. He tears off his wife beater before tossing it away. All of his smooth, tattooed muscles are on full display. My mouth waters for him. Then, he unbuckles his jeans. He pushes them and his boxers down his thighs. His thick, veiny cock bobs out in front of me. Heavy and glistening at the tip. Arousal seeps from him.

He loves danger too.

"I want to touch you," I say with a pout.

He strokes my hair before he gathers it in his fists. "That's your punishment. You can't use your hands."

I groan when he rocks his hips from side to side, his large cock slapping against my cheeks. His El Malo tattoo is revealed on his lower torso and the devil's tail that curls from the "o" points straight at his cock. I love this tattoo. It may represent his evilness, but it's so damn mesmerizing.

Leaning forward, I seek out his erection. My lip stings when I open my mouth wide to accommodate his thickness. He pulls on my hair gently and I look up at him. Wild lust has transformed his features. Gone is the fierce mobster and in his place is a beast. A beast that wants to feed on me. Me, his willing victim.

I drag my attention back to his dark, pubic hair that's been buzzed short. With my lips wide open, I bring my mouth down around his massive cock. I barely get past the crown before my teeth are scraping against him. He hisses but not from pain or fear. Javier loves this.

Groaning, I try to open my mouth wider. Ever since Michael hit me, my jaw has been swollen and sore. But I don't care that it hurts. I want to take Javier as deep as I can go.

"Need some help, *mami*?" Javier croons.

"Mmhmm," I moan in response around his flesh.

He grips my hair and starts force feeding me his cock. It's too big and my mouth is inclined to close around him. I can barely breathe and my gag reflex makes my throat constrict. Tears and snot stream as I struggle to breathe.

"Fuck," he snarls, the tip of his cock pushing into my throat. I can feel my teeth scraping against him, but he's fearless. "Fuck, my sweet Rosa. Fuck."

The very idea that I have this strong, terrifying villain losing control has me delirious with pleasure. I gag and sputter around him, but I let him use me to feel good. It makes me feel good. I'm already dripping wet between my thighs at the wonder of what will happen next. Will he facefuck me until I pass out?

He pushes my head all the way against him. My nostrils are smashed against his pubic hairs. I can't breathe or move or think. All I can do is give in to the monster. Black clouds of lust and desperation swirl around me.

I'm his.

I'm his.

I'm his.

Despite the fact I'm completely at his mercy, I trust him. A monster. The monster. I trust him more than I ever trusted Michael. He pulls away sharply and I dry heave. I suck in air that smells like him, getting high on the scent. Then, he's pushing back inside my mouth. He skullfucks me hard and furiously until I'm on the edge of blacking out.

"Oh, Rosa, you goddamned perfect woman," he bellows before yanking out of me.

His hand wraps around his cock and he jerks himself until his hot streams of cum spurt on my messy face. I'm so under his spell and desperate for him, I open my mouth, eager to taste him. Saltiness lands on my tongue and I greedily drink it down. Most of it lands on my face and eyelids. When he's done coming, he staggers backward, nearly falling with his pants at his knees now. He bends and hastily jerks them up before he dives his hand into his pocket.

When he pulls out the knife, I don't even flinch. He could plunge it into my neck right now and I wouldn't even care, as long as he was the one to do it.

I've fallen.

I've fallen so hard for this man and I'll never get back up.

In the deep, dark depths of hell is where I belong, it would seem.

He walks behind me and proceeds to saw through my bindings. When I'm free, he hooks an arm around me and hauls me to my feet.

"Sweet, perfect Rosa," he murmurs as he scoops me into his arms. "Let me clean you up, *mami*."

I close my eyes and smile.

I'm lost, so lost, but he keeps finding me.

Over and over again.

The rest of the world doesn't matter.

It's just him and me.

Capítulo Dieciséis

Javier

I stare at her and wonder how it came to this. It's been nearly two months since Michael raped her. This entire time hunting and not finding that dirty bastard. What I have found are pieces of a puzzle. A picture that's becoming clear before my very eyes.

Deception.

Betrayal.

Lies.

And yet, I stare at her from across the dinner table, salivating for her. She's a little weaver of lies and I can't look away. I let her lie to me. I fucking like it. It fuels me like a shot of heroin to the system. I'm always high from it. Just waiting for it all to unravel.

She can't lie forever.

One day, all her secrets will be laid before me.

I'll be forced to cut her open and watch her bleed.

I may as well cut my motherfucking soul out when that happens.

Fuck her for doing this to me.

Fuck her for digging in so deep, threading herself into my entire being. She's in everything. Seeps from my pores. Saturates my cock. Infects my mind.

An illness I'll never recover from.

I'll die from her.

A broken heart is real.

My father nearly died of one when my mother died.

I have no doubt it'll be the same for me.

"It's so warm today," she says, a smile tilting her full red lips. Her head is turned to look out at the ocean. The black strapless dress hugs her curves in a way that has every male in the vicinity turning his head to look at her. All it takes is seeing who she's with before they're quickly looking away.

She's mine.

The thought is possessive and maddening.

I'm fucking crazy over her.

My duties to my father—to El Malo—fall by the wayside because I can't get her out of my head.

"Great day for a swim," I muse aloud.

She nods before turning back to me. Her fingers nervously twist her bracelet around her wrist. It's one of the many I've gifted her. Even liars deserve to feel pretty. Her brows furrow together and she won't meet my eyes.

"After dinner, I wanted to stop off at one of the shops." She swallows and her hand shakes. "To buy you a gift."

Liar. Liar. Fucking liar. "Of course, *manzanita*. I suppose it's a surprise?"

Her brown eyes lift to mine and she nods. How can someone lie straight to your face and look so innocent about it? Does she believe the shit she spews? I sure as fuck don't. It's my job to sniff out liars and expose them. I'm good at it. It has taken some unraveling, but I'm peeling Rosa apart piece by piece until I get to the center. I'm so close.

"I won't be gone long," she promises. "I think you'll love it."

I lift my hand and wave the server over to bring me the check. She's so eager to deceive me. I'll help her along. The quicker we get to that point, the better. I'm not into torture unlike my victims who visit the shed from time to time. I fucking hate torture. Especially the emotional kind. It's worse than any blade or tool. She's cutting my heart out day by day.

And yet I can't hate her.

It's the opposite, in fact.

For once, I'm deluded about what I should do. I don't dare speak of these things to my father or my men. I certainly don't say them to her. I just sit and stew and ponder the fuck out of our future.

We have no future.

"Are you okay?" she asks, genuine concern in her eyes.

No, Rosa, I'm not okay. You're fucking me over and I'm letting you.

"Perfect, *mami*."

She frowns as if she doesn't believe me but doesn't say another word on the subject. I pay the tab and stand. She takes my offered hand and I pull her up. With her purse clutched protectively at her side, she wraps her arm around mine and leans her head on my shoulder.

An ache, deep in my chest, won't stop throbbing as we walk out of the hotel restaurant and out onto the street. I let her guide me past some shops that haven't been ravaged by crime until she stops in front of an old shop. One of those shops that sells anything and everything. I wonder who she's meeting here because there's nothing I could ever want or need from a place like this.

"I'll be right back." Her bright smile is disarming. She's so fucking good. I lean down to accept a kiss on the mouth.

Before she can get too far, I grab her waist and pull her to me. Her eyes are soft and loving as she regards me. "Don't go," I utter, my words so quiet you can barely hear them over the busy shoppers chattering as they walk by.

This moment feels pivotal.

I can sense it with every fiber of my being.

"Javier," she murmurs. "What's gotten into you? Are you feeling okay?"

I hug her to me and inhale her hair. For a minute, we simply hold one another. Of all my abilities to get this town to yield to my demands, why can't freezing time be one of them? Long before I'm ready, she pulls away.

"I'll be right back. I promise. Then, we can go back home and get back in bed," she says, her cheeks turning slightly pink.

Reaching forward, I clutch her neck in a possessive way before pressing my lips to hers. Her kiss is tentative at first but then she kisses me with so much passion it confuses me. She lies even to herself. One doesn't kiss like that unless they want to.

Sweet, confused Rosa.

She pulls away and I watch her rush inside the building. I'm left alone on the sidewalk, wishing for more time.

Unfortunately, time has officially run out.

Capítulo Diecisiete

Rosa

I don't know what's gotten into Javier, but it makes me nervous. I'm questioning what to do next.

He's a killer.

When he finds out I'm with the CIA sent to track his every movement, he'll no doubt kill me. He's told me without saying those exact words. It will happen.

The woman in me craves to simply ignore my duties. Play pretend. Act as though I never worked for the agency. That I was always a little ol' maid.

"May I use your phone?" I croak out to the cashier.

He's old and seems used to the request because he hands me a portable. "If you're calling long distance, I'll need to know the number so I can look up the cost to bill you."

I give him a clipped nod. "United States."

"Make your call," he grunts.

With shaking hands, I start to dial the number I was forced to memorize. Agent Stokes' number. I'm to call him the moment I can. Those were his orders over four years ago. If I lost contact with Michael, I was to get ahold of them when I could. I'm still baffled as to how come they haven't swooped in to save me. It's as though everyone is holding their collective breath, waiting for just a few more scraps of information. I'm assuming Michael didn't tell them he raped me, so maybe they don't even know I've lost contact. Whatever it is, I need to get ahold of them and see.

I can't go on like this forever.

Now, too much is at stake.

I'm stuck in limbo and it's not fair to any of us.

With tears in my eyes, I dial the number. Before I hit the last number, I hit the end button. I can't do this. Thoughts of flying back to the US, working at a desk in Langley, spending every night alone while Javier sits in jail weighs heavily on me.

I don't want that.

Not at all.

Sniffling, I hand the phone back to him. I browse the store and find what I want to purchase. It doesn't cost me much and I shove it into my purse. Taking a deep breath, I swipe my tears and head outside. I find Javier not waiting for me on foot but inside his Thunderbird. The sun catches the red paint job and sparkles like glitter. He's absolutely breathtaking seated on the white leather. A picture of perfection.

Mine.

But he doesn't look at me.

His focus is straight ahead, his jaw set. I climb in beside him and clutch my purse tightly.

"I got it," I squeak out and smile at him.

He doesn't reply as he guns it. I quickly fasten my seatbelt as panic rises in my chest. Did he see me calling? He has no idea who I'd be calling. I'm freaking out for no reason.

"I want to show you someplace special," he says, his voice cold and lacking inflection. He glances my way, but I can't see his eyes hidden behind his fashionable sunglasses.

I reach for his hand, but he grips the steering wheel with both hands, denying our connection. "Javier, what's going on? You're scaring me."

He flashes me a smile, but it doesn't reveal his dimple. It's not the good kind of smile. It's the kind of smile that feels threatening.

"I want to go home," I choke out.

"Do you now?"

"Yes. Let's just go home and get in the hot tub."

He turns down a street that's lined with trees. A kid runs out into the street after a red ball and he slows to let them pass. Then, he drives until we come to a clearing blocked off by several big rocks.

"Get out," he snaps.

I jolt at his harsh words. He climbs out of the car and stalks to the clearing. I set my purse down and follow after him. Up here on this cliff, the winds are high and my hair blows all around, whipping me in the face. I follow him to the edge where he stands, looking over, with his hands on his narrow hips. In his pale gray slacks and linen white button-down shirt, he's handsome as ever.

"What's wrong?" I ask, my voice getting lost in the wind.

"Thirty meters," he tells me as he points to the churning ocean at the bottom of the cliff. "Thirty meters from here to there."

Panic flitters through me as I peer over the ledge. I

grow dizzy at the height and clutch his elbow.

"We're too close," I choke out.

He turns toward me and tosses his glasses into the grass. "You've been lying to me, Rosa. Admit it."

I gape at him in shock. "W-What?"

"About everything. You're not Rosa Delgado, are you?"

Holding up my hands, I start stammering. "L-Listen. I am Rosa."

He grips my wrists and pulls me to him. His eyes flash with a mixture of fury and heartbreak. My own heart cracks open in the process. "How can you lie straight to my face?" he demands, his voice harsh.

"I. Am. Rosa."

He blinks in confusion. "I don't matter to you. You have a hidden agenda."

Not anymore.

"No," I rasp out over the wind. "You matter to me. You're everything to me, Javier." Tears pool and then spill from my lids.

His brows furl together and he's so visibly upset, I let out a choked sob on his behalf. The big, brave, fierce El Malo leader is broken. I broke him.

"I don't understand how you can look me right in the eyes and tell these lies." His jaw clenches and his Adam's apple bobs as he swallows down his emotion.

I try to clutch onto his lapels, but his grip on my wrists is too strong. "Javier, please," I beg. "Please listen to me." He's blurry through my tears, but I blurt out the words I've wanted to say for a long time. "I love you. I love you so much it hurts. It tears me in half. Right down the middle. I'm so lost and confused but somehow, with you, everything makes perfect sense."

"Lies," he roars over the wind, one of his arms wrapping around my waist.

"Not lies!" I shriek. "I've loved you from the moment you made me yours."

He growls and presses his forehead to mine. Fire and fury blazes in his gaze. "If you love me like you claim, would you die for me?"

My heart sinks. I'd rather live.

But without him, my world feels empty. Going back to my life when Javier wasn't mine and I was just drifting through the motions feels like torture. Every bit as awful as the shed. I didn't realize what a ghost I'd become. I was hell-bent on seeking vengeance for what happened to my mother that I didn't care it came at the expense of my happiness.

I was never happy.

The last time I was truly happy was when I skipped my way into that restaurant when I was a young girl. Before my happiness was stolen from me in the blink of an eye. It didn't return until a couple of months ago when I somehow got dragged right to the center of Javier's world.

And I am happy.

"I would die for you," I tell him honestly.

His fierce features fall as he regards me in confusion. He releases my wrist but holds my waist tightly. Gently, he runs his nose along mine and then kisses my lips. "Then we will both die because I can't live without you, *manzanita*."

I don't understand the violent change in our afternoon, but I know exactly how he feels. I cling to his solid frame, seeking out his comfort.

"If you tell me the truth, you can go. You don't love me," he says, bitterness in his tone. "You can walk away. But if you love me like you claim, you're sentencing us both to death." He points to the water below that churns wildly. "Millions of big, sharp rocks. Say the words and you may leave. I'm giving you your out."

I tilt my head up and meet his stare. Then, I stand on my toes and kiss his mouth. "I love you, Javier Estrada, and you can't talk me out of it."

He growls. "I love you too, Rosa. Forgive me."

With those words, he tightens his grip around me and then he leaps. Straight off the cliff. His body wraps around mine and his legs tangle with mine pinning them. My stomach is left on the ledge as we sail toward our deaths.

All I can think about is him.

Crash!

I expect instant death. Exploding bones. Not this. Not ice-cold waters and being plunged so deep I wonder if it ever ends. The waves yank me away from Javier and I thrash in the blinding dark depths as I try to figure which way is up. My lungs protest, aching to breathe, as I swim hard in no direction whatsoever. I believe I truly will die when a strong arm snags my middle.

Javier.

My savior.

He swims hard and powerfully in a direction that must be the correct one. And soon, my lungs get the fresh air they so desperately crave. I suck in a deep breath before a wave topples us once more. But this time, he doesn't let go. He swims with me in his grip until my feet kick up gravel beneath the surface.

Land.

I'm weak and still gasping for air as he scoops me in his strong arms. He carries me to a warm, sandy area and sets me down. Before I can argue, he pounces on me. Our mouths crash together in a painful way as he lays me flat, his hands ripping my dress up.

"Javier," I say, sobbing. "Javier."

"I know," he croons. "I love you too. I had to be sure."

His cock is out and he pushes my panties to the side. With a quick, hard thrust, he drives into me. I latch onto his hair and dig my heels into his ass. He fucks me hard and without apology right on the banks of the water. His grunts and groans are claiming and animalistic.

I need him.

I can't live without him.

My crying becomes overwhelming. I almost ruined it all. I almost called in to the CIA and would have lost him. I would have killed us figuratively.

I'm too selfish.

I'll keep him until they rip me from his arms.

There's no other way.

I don't orgasm. It's not about that in this moment. It's just about being connected to someone in a way you've never been in your entire life. I claw at him and kiss him desperately. With a guttural sound, he comes. His thrusting becomes uneven and harsh until he falls against me.

"Rosa," he says fiercely, his dark eyes finding mine. Panic flashes in them. Heartache. Loss.

"I'm here," I choke out.

"I had to be sure," he murmurs, water dripping from his hair and face. He looks so young and terrified. It kills me. "I had to be sure. Rosa, I had to be sure."

I nod as tears leak out. "I know. I know, Javi, I know."

"What is this place?" I ask as we pull up to a nondescript building. It's dark and the only signs of life are a neon orange sign that boasts "open" on the brick wall.

"You'll see." He gives my hand a reassuring squeeze before he climbs out of the Thunderbird.

Earlier, we spent hours drying out and making love on the sandy banks. He revealed that those cliffs are ones he's familiar with. Cliffs he's jumped from hundreds of times. My safety was never at stake, but our future was. Because of his position in this country, he can't trust just anyone. He shouldn't trust me. But he does and I'll be damned if I screw this up. Not now.

He opens the car door and helps me out. I clutch my purse in one hand and take his hand in the other. We're both dry now. I look a fright with my messy hair and missing shoes that are now at the bottom of the ocean, but with the adoring way Javier regards me, I don't care.

"Estrada," a man hoots as we walk inside. The man is tall, much taller than Javier, and scary. He has more tattoos than anyone I've ever seen. His eyes are completely white, thanks to contacts, and when he grins, he reveals sharpened teeth. The man has more piercings on his face than I think humanly possible, but here he is. Looking like a total freak show. It should unnerve me, but Javier shakes his hand and then pats his back.

"Facundo and I used to run around together when we were kids," Javier explains. "His father is friends with mine." Javier points to me. "Facundo, this is my Rosa."

I shake his hand and let out a nervous giggle when he kisses the back of my hand. "Nice to meet you, Facundo."

He releases me and then holds his hands in the air. "What'll it be?"

"I want a neck tattoo right here," Javier tells him and drags his finger along his flesh that is unmarred by ink. "Want anything, Rosa?"

I want to prove my loyalty to him, but I have a few questions.

"Maybe…" I murmur, chewing on my bottom lip.

Javier smirks at me. "Think about it, *mami*. I'm going to take a piss. Don't let her out of your sight and keep her safe."

Facundo nods. "Yep."

As soon as he's gone, I rush out with a million different questions for Facundo. He's very professional and answers them all honestly. My nerves take a backseat.

"Are you sure it's safe?" I ask again.

He chuckles. "Positively. *No te preocupes, cariño.*" *Don't worry, sweetheart.*

Javier emerges from the bathroom, drying his hands with a paper towel. He tosses the trash and then unbuttons his shirt. Before he peels it away, I stop him.

"I'm going first," I tell him bravely. "Facundo is going to tattoo me."

Javier's brows lift in surprise. "Is that so, *manzanita*? Are you sure? Tattoos are a lifelong commitment."

I snort. "Okay, Dad."

His grin is wolfish. "Call me daddy and you can have

187

whatever you want."

"You two are kinky as fuck, aren't you?" Facundo asks. *"Muy caliente."* So hot. "Sit there, Javi, and she's going to straddle you. It'll make it easier for what she wants."

Javier obliges and sits down on the bench that's at a forty-five degree angle. I straddle his narrow waist and run my palms up his now bare chest. His shirt hangs from the side, but all his muscled tattooed goodness is available for my touch.

"Take your dress off," Facundo commands. "It'll just get in the way."

Javier's eyes are laser sharp as he watches me peel away my dress in front of another man. Facundo seems uninterested behind me as he readies his supplies. Javier pulls me against him so my bare breasts smash against his smooth flesh. I rest my ear on his chest, loving how I can hear the steady beat of his heart. Behind me, I feel Facundo pushing down my panties some with his latex gloved hands. Then, he starts cleaning the area. I close my eyes and breathe through my fraying nerves.

This is it.

I've become completely his.

The buzzing of the gun soothes my nerves until the bite of the tattoo gun stings me. I hiss in pain and Javier strokes my hair in a comforting way.

"Relax, *mami*, I have you."

For once, the worries always plaguing me are gone. I curl against the man I love's chest and relax to the sound of Facundo's whistling.

I'm doing this.

I am El Malo.

Capítulo Dieciocho

Javier

"**M**ami," I murmur, kissing down Rosa's spine as she sleeps. She grumbles and I chuckle against her flesh. "So grumpy." When I get to her tattoo, pride surges through me. It's been nearly a week since we got them and they look fucking awesome. Especially hers. Beautiful.

I grip her fleshy ass and spread her cheeks apart. Not a day goes by where I don't wake up with her on my mind. Eager to be inside her. Fucking what's mine throughout the day because I can.

"You're supposed to let me sleep," she whines.

Spreading her thighs with my knee, I ease myself behind her. I rub the tip of my cock along her cunt and am pleased she's only been pretending to sleep. She's slick and ready, just like always. Slowly, I push into her tight body. Her hands fist the sheets and she moans at the intrusion.

"Sleep, Rosa," I tease as I thrust into her. "I'll do all the work."

She giggles and her cunt clenches around me. "You're crazy."

I start nipping at her shoulder until she squeals. She squirms, but I don't let her get away. While I'm still inside of her, I roll onto my back. We both groan at the way it feels to be inside her this way. She bends her knees and keeps her feet flat on the bed. I buck my hips from beneath her, loving the groans coming from her.

"Touch your pussy, *manzanita*," I growl. "Make yourself come because these titties are begging for attention."

She whimpers when I grope her fat tits. I fuck her from beneath her, listening intently to the way she sounds as she pleasures herself. Sweet groans and soft moans. So fucking hot.

Her body trembles as she chases her morning orgasm. So close. I nip at her skin and whisper dirty things against her hair near her ear. She comes with a loud, appreciative sound and milks my cock.

"Oh, *mami*, you're going to be the death of me. Your body is so fucking hot and mine," I croon as I roll us to our side. I pull out of her cunt and stroke my cock. "You know what I want?"

"What?" she rasps out.

I hike her thigh up over mine, opening her up to me and then grip my cock again. It's soaked from being inside of her. Still, though, I could use for more lubricant. I spit on my fingers and rub them against the puckered hole of her ass. She likes it when I get adventurous and today I'm feeling really goddamn adventurous. Her hole is tight and resistant to my entry, but I'm patient. Slowly, with gentle pushes, I urge it open for me. The moment the crown of my cock presses into her, her body relaxes and I'm sucked the rest of the way in.

Sweet motherfucking bliss.

El Malo

Her ass is heaven.

Each time I take her here, I lose my damn mind. At first, she cried. My cock is large and her body is small. A fat dick in your ass is painful. But after some practice, she's doing so well.

"That's it," I croon against her ear as I slide my hand to her tit and pinch her nipple. "I own all your holes, *mami*."

"Yesss," she breathes. "Oh, God."

Sliding my hand down between her thighs, I push two fingers into her hot cunt that still drips with pleasure. I fuck her with my fingers in tandem with the way I roughly grind into her ass. She's losing her mind too. Her claws dig into my forearm as she rocks with me. Garbled pleas and orders stream from her lips, but nothing makes sense. All that makes sense is how fucking good we are together.

"Feel me inside every part of you?" I murmur. "I'm stealing your soul."

She moans, her ass squeezing my cock so hard I nearly black out from the pure orgasmic pleasure of it. I pinch her nipple and thrust harder.

"Who do you belong to?" I grit out, my control unraveling with every second that passes.

"You," she cries out. "Only you."

I come with a harsh breath and my seed spurts deep inside her ass. My cum will run out of her for hours to come, much to her embarrassment and much to my motherfucking delight. She's not concerned about that right now, though. Right now, she's bucking against my fingers, desperate for that deep orgasm only her sweet G-spot will deliver. I fuck her just right with my hand until she convulses. My softening cock gets strangled back to life when she orgasms, her entire body seizing up violently.

This thing between us is utterly maddening.

Completely consuming.

A total mindfuck.

"I love you, goddammit," I snarl against her sweaty neck. "I love you so much it makes me insane."

She relaxes in my grip and her ass naturally pushes my cock out of her. We make a big fucking mess all over the sheets that she'll fret about later. Right now she's languid in my arms.

"You know I love you," she murmurs.

That I do.

The music thumps and the party is hopping. People are everywhere. Rosa is by the food table outside looking way too delicious to be standing alone. She keeps popping grapes into her mouth as she dances. I take a moment to admire her juicy ass in her fitted red dress. It's short and revealing and makes my dick hard every time she walks by. I'm about to attack my girl when I notice Angel messing with one of the maids. Araceli is her name. Because of Rosa, I now know all their names and speak to them from time to time.

I whistle to gain his attention. He doesn't seem to hear, but she does. She starts to back away, but he grabs her wrist, tugging her closer. Her worried gaze is on me, especially now that I'm stalking their way. She manages to jerk her arm free and scurries away.

"What's the status on Michael?" I demand, startling him.

He twists around and flinches upon seeing me. Good. Fucker needs to remember whose roof he's under. "Working on it, *jefe*. I am confident we'll find him. I've been working this city from every angle, dangling that reward in their faces. They're all practically salivating as they hunt for that fucker."

I give him a nod. "Excellent. Remember, I want him alive."

Leaving Angel, I prowl outside to where Rosa dances. I sneak up behind her and then grab her hips. Together, our hips move with the upbeat song. She gathers up her long, wavy, dark brown hair and holds it up on top of her head. I take the opportunity to let my palms roam all over her curvy body. Her ass jiggles as she rocks it against my aching dick. The woman knows how to bring a grown man to his knees on the dance floor with her exotic dance moves. I'm practically coming in my slacks at the way she rubs against me.

"Your ass is a sin," I tell her, my fingers biting into her hips. She looks like heaven with a sinful body. "I can't take you dancing like this, *mami*. You'll make me embarrass the both of us if you're not careful."

She looks over her shoulder and grins. "Then maybe we should take the party someplace private." She dances in place in a circle until she's facing me. Her dress is a low-cut halter that shows so much fucking cleavage. I want to pour the finest tequila between her tits and lap it away until I'm drunk as fuck.

"Eyes up here," she teases.

I lean forward and bite part of her tit that's on full

display. "Who says I'm interested in those eyes."

Her fingers thread into my hair and she lets out a soft moan. "Javi…"

She drives me mad when she says my name that way.

"Yes, *manzanita*?"

"Get me out of here."

I grip her wrist and guide her back into my house. She clomps behind me in her sexy-as-hell stilettoes. I want them digging into me the next time I fuck her, which is looking like soon. We make it to my room and she reaches into my pocket, pulling my phone from inside. Long ago, I wouldn't have trusted her, but now I do. She unlocks my phone and hunts for a song. When she puts "Despacito" on, I start laughing.

"Oh, shit," I say, grinning. "It's your song."

"Damn right," she replies, flashing me a sultry smile.

As the music thumps, she begins stripping. Something I'll never grow tired of. Her fingers untie the knot at the back of her neck and she slowly peels the dress down her body. I'm mesmerized when she bares her tits to me. As she dances, they bounce. So fucking hot. She continues her striptease and works the material down to her hips. Then, she pushes it past her flared hips, letting the dress fall to the floor. Her panties are a simple red thong. I want to rip it off with my teeth. When I growl at her, she waggles a finger at me.

"Not so fast," she says and steps out of her dress. With her dark hair hanging in front of her shoulders, her lips a blood red, her fake lashes long and sexy as hell, and her tits on full display as she stands in nothing but panties and fuck-me heels, I start to lose my motherfucking mind.

"Three seconds and then I'm taking you against that wall," I warn. "Make it quick, whatever it is."

She smiles sweetly at me, such a stark contrast to her seductive look. "Stay right there. I have a present for you."

I yank at the knot of my tie as she turns and bares her round ass at me. The tattoo on her lower back in black ink is perfect. She waltzes over to her side of the dresser and opens a drawer. I manage to pull off my jacket and shirt while she digs around under her bras and panties in the drawer. I'm just unbuckling my pants when she hides something behind her back.

Arching a brow at her, I chuckle. "What is it?"

Her cheeks turn bright red. "Do you remember when I wanted to go to that shop?"

Guilt surges through me. That was the day I jumped the cliff with her. "I just wanted to be sure," I mutter again.

Her smile is breathtaking. "I know, baby. But before you were making me prove my love to you, I had a present for you." She steps my way and her tits bounce along the way, making my mouth water. "Here." When she holds up a cigar, I frown.

Not just any cigar but one that's made of chewing gum.

"Nice," I lie. What the fuck do I want a chewing gum cigar for?

She laughs. "Read it, Javi."

I pluck it from her hand and twist it around. "Congratulations," I read aloud. Still, I don't get why the fuck she's giving me this shit. "Um, thanks?"

"Oh my God," she says with a groan. "Maybe this

will make you understand." She hands me a white plastic stick.

Taking it from her, I stare down at in wonder. This one, I don't miss the meaning at all. It's evident from the get-go.

Pregnant.

"I took a test last week and another to be sure this morning, but, Javi, we're going to have a baby," she tells me, her smile widening.

I toss the test and the cigar to the floor before grabbing her hips, yanking her to me. My lips crash to hers and I kiss her until she's moaning against my mouth. Gripping her by the ass, I lift her and walk her to the very wall I intend on fucking her against. Except when I make it there, I don't move. Simply press her back to the wall and stare at her.

"¿Voy a ser papá?" *I will be a daddy?*

She nods, tears welling in her eyes. "*Sí.*"

I maul her, eager to show her just how happy I am when she palms my scruffy cheeks. Her eyes are sad and serious. "You don't doubt my love, do you?"

"*Nunca más.*" *Never again.*

"*Bien.*" *Good.*

She pulls me closer so her lips brush against my ear. I'm drunk on her news, but her whispered words sober me up. I listen to every single syllable and inflection. Catalogue them all and record them away.

And when she's done…

I pull her thong to the side and fuck the love of my life.

Capítulo Diecinueve

Rosa

Three months later...

The blanket Leticia knitted is soft and I can't stop touching it. My heart swells that she put so much time and effort into the gift for our baby.

Baby.

I can hardly believe it.

I'm pregnant with Javier Estrada's child and couldn't be happier about it. I fold the blanket and set it in the crib. The nursery is coming together nicely. We've chosen to keep the sex a secret even though the doctor told us she knows the sex. As long as the baby is healthy, we're happy. It's just a waiting game at this point. In about four more months, our family will be complete.

With a happy sigh, I finish readying the room and then leave. I run right into the solid brick wall that is Angel. He steadies me by grabbing my biceps and the metal of his brass knuckles bites into my flesh. I flash a fake smile—for him and not the hidden cameras that watch our every move. Truth is, he makes me nervous. I don't like how he seems to stalk Araceli. She assures me she can handle it, but I still worry over my girls. They may not work directly for me like they used to, but they're still my friends. Araceli is like the little sister I never had. The thought of him roughing her up has me angry on her behalf.

"Nice dress," he says, his pupils wide with whatever it is he's on as of late. He doesn't release me and I don't jerk away from him. Angel thrives on intimidating women. Unfortunately, his tactics don't work on me.

In this home, I am safe.

With Javier, I am safe.

I glower up at him. "Thanks."

His gaze lingers at my cleavage. My breasts are much fuller being that I'm pregnant and Angel doesn't seem to miss that fact. Ever. Although, he attempts to keep his eyes to himself whenever Javier is near.

But Javier misses nothing.

"If you're done eye-fucking my tits, I'd like to go lie down before dinner with Javier tonight," I bark out, leveling him with a hard glare.

He smirks, confident and arrogant, but removes his hands from me. The asshole makes a blatant show of checking out my breasts a few moments longer. Bold and brave this one. "*Jefe* wants you to wear a sexy dress and then I'm to drive you. He says he has something real special planned for you."

I give him a clipped nod and slip into our bedroom beside the baby's room. Turning the lock behind me, I breathe a sigh of relief knowing I'm alone. I rummage around in our closet until I find a new maternity dress Javier hasn't seen yet that I bought online. Using Javier's computer. A computer that even though he gave me the password and tempted me at one time with potential new information, I never abused by snooping. Just shopping.

My dress is beautiful. It's sunshine yellow and hugs all my curves. I like it because it's sleeveless, low cut, and short. I won't get too sweaty in it. Once I put on some glitzy jewelry and step into my wedge sandals, I apply some makeup and curl my hair into the sexy waves he loves so much. Finally, I spritz on some perfume and decide I look as sexy as a pregnant woman can be.

Tears prickle my eyes as I clutch my rounded belly. It's as though someone placed a small basketball inside me. I can hardly believe life grows within me.

"Time to go," Angel barks from the other side of the door.

His tone irritates me, but I blow it off for now. I'm ready to see Javier anyway. Angel's eyes bug out of his head when he rakes his gaze over my appearance.

"Fuck, *jefe* is so lucky." He scratches at his jaw, his stupid brass knuckles still attached to his fingers, as he smirks. "You and me could run away, baby. Leave right now. I could make all your dreams come true."

"You're pushing it," I snap and push past him. "Rein it in, asshole."

He growls a "fucking whatever" before he storms past me. I lift my chin and walk after him, taking my time. When I get to the carport, he's waiting beside his cherry red Mustang that Javi bought for his undeserving ass. Javier spoils everyone in his life who are loyal to him.

The ones who are not…

They die.

A shudder ripples past me, but I shake it away. Javier

and I are fine. We're more than fine. We're perfect. I settle into the passenger seat as Angel fires up the obnoxiously loud engine. He backs out of the driveway past the estate gates and barrels through town.

Away from the restaurants.

Away from the hotels.

Away from the city.

We're going to the shed.

The last time I was at the shed, I'd been disgusted at seeing that man strapped to the chair. Javier turned into a maniac before my very eyes. It was frightening to watch. But necessary. Sometimes we have to do horrible things to bad people. No matter how scary or disgusting or soulless. It must be done because if we don't take out the trash, they'll hurt the ones we love.

"Javier is here?" I ask as we pull up in front of the industrial building beside Alejandro's Hummer and Marco Antonio's Land Rover.

Angel puts the car in park and flashes me an evil stare. "He is and he's called to meet you here."

He climbs out of the car and seconds later, he's at my side. Roughly, he grabs my bicep and yanks me to my feet.

"Ow!" I hiss at him. "Don't touch me."

"Sorry, baby, I've got orders." The smug bastard grips me hard as he drags me to the door. He rings the buzzer and someone lets him in. I know the password to get in but certainly don't offer that information to him.

Javier won't like the way he's touching me.

He's walking a slippery slope here.

I'm all but dragged to the room where they torture people. My heart rate spikes and I try to pull away. Angel finally releases me and steps to the side.

Marco Antonio, Alejandro, and Arturo all stand along the wall with AK-47s in their hands, all matching in their black suits. Their faces are somber. They won't look at me.

Ice clutches around my heart. Someone sits on a chair in the middle of the room and I can't look at him. No, my gaze seeks out the one I love. Javier. He is an avenging angel in a cream-colored Ermenegildo Zegna Bespoke custom-tailored suit. It hugs his perfect body in all the right places. The pale-yellow dress shirt he wears beneath it compliments my dress and brings out his tan skin tones. My name, scrawled in red and black ink, is tattooed beautifully on his neck over a blooming red rose. I never grow tired of looking at it.

"Hi, baby," I croak out, my voice stolen by nerves.

His icy stare bores into me. No smile. No dimple. No love flaring in his dark brown eyes. Before me doesn't stand the man. He is the monster. El Malo. Terrifyingly beautiful.

"Rosa," he greets, his voice cold.

Breathe, Rosa.

He loves you.

Even with those words replaying in my mind, it doesn't make the shed any less horrifying.

His gaze falls to my stomach that holds his child. I expect a break in his fearsome stare, but instead he lingers his eyes for a moment before he looks elsewhere. Like a hurricane in a small room, he stalks past me to where his beloved apron hangs on the wall. He slides it on over his head and then gestures to the chair.

I reluctantly address the elephant in the room. There,

sitting in the chair, is my worst nightmare. CIA Agent Michael Stiner. Naked. Sweaty. Bound. His mouth is secured by a strip of duct tape. Sandy-blond hair is sticking up everywhere, accentuating his bald spot. He's heavier than I remember. Man boobs hanging on his chest. A fat gut sitting on his thighs. His cock remains unharmed. For now. It peeks out from beneath his stomach, flaccid and unimpressive, no longer a threat to me as his reddish-blond pubes that are overgrown and unkempt seem to want to swallow it whole.

Memories of that night assault me. The pain I felt when he hit me with the tequila bottle. The fist to my jaw. His brutality as he fucked me against my will. Back when his cock was a threat to me. I shudder and choke down the bile rising in my throat.

"Javier," I whimper. Suddenly, I don't feel so brave at all.

His murderous stare finds mine. I'd like to think his fury isn't aimed at me. It's aimed at Michael. But all Javier's normal tells are missing. I don't really know this man in the rubber apron. He's from another realm—one I've never been to.

"What happens when you touch Javier Estrada's girl?" Javier asks, his piercing stare never leaving me.

His men answer in unison behind him. "You die."

Javier picks up an ice pick from the tool chest and walks over to Michael, who watches him with wide, fearful eyes. I hold my breath, wondering what he'll do. At one time, I would have tried to stop him.

Not now.

Javier grabs the corner of the tape and rips it away from Michael's mouth.

"Rosa," he calls out to me. "Rosa, help me!"

Panic rises up inside me and I find myself backing up. I slam right into Angel, who grips my biceps and holds me in place, his hard fingers punishing my flesh. Javier has his back to me, but Marco Antonio keeps a sharp, watchful eye on me.

Don't freak out.

Don't freak out.

I'm freaking out.

"What happens when you touch Javier Estrada's girl?" Javier demands again, this time his question directed at Michael.

"No, man," Michael defends. "She was my girlfriend and—" A howl pierces the air when Javier plunges the ice pick into the side of Michael's arm. He leaves it there and turns to glower at me.

The intensity rippling from him has my knees buckling. Angel grips me harder until I let out a yelp, but I don't fall.

"You fucked him because you wanted to or because he forced you?" Javier demands. He knows the answer, but I remind him again.

"H-He hurt me. He held me down and…" I trail off, tears welling.

Javier's jaw clenches and he turns to regard Michael again. "You're a liar, you fat fuck. Do you know what I do to liars?" He yanks the ice pick out of Michael's arm and then slams it into his thigh.

"Fuck!" Michael screams. "Stop fucking stabbing me!" Michael turns his hate-filled glare my way. "What you do to me you have to do to her," he spits out. "I'm not the only liar around here."

That asshole.

This goes against everything the agency taught us.

You don't sell out your own people.

"No, Michael," I whine.

Angel laughs from behind me, his brutal grip no doubt bruising my arms. Marco Antonio's glare is punishing, but he makes no moves to stop him. If looks could kill, though...

"My sweet *manzanita*? A liar?" Javier asks, his shoulders tense.

Like a bobble head, Michael nods. "C-Check my bag. I have her passport. She's Agent Rosa Daza with the motherfucking CIA!" The evil look of smug satisfaction he shoots my way makes me want to throw up.

Javier won't look at me. Instead, he points to the bag. "Angel, let's see if Michael is telling the truth."

"Don't fucking think about walking out of here or those big motherfuckers over there will mow you down with those AKs," Angel hisses against my ear before releasing me.

I rub my palms up and down my biceps and bow my head. My skin feels cold. My heart is going numb. The tears that threaten to fall are barely kept at bay.

Javier loves you.

Everything will be okay.

"Holy fuck, *jefe*. Look at this shit," Angel says as he tosses my passport at Javier.

The room goes deathly quiet for a moment. Then, I hear Javier's shoes squeak across the floor until his powerful form is just inches from mine. I'm still looking down so my passport comes into view before he does.

"Who is this?" Javier demands, his voice a low,

threatening growl.

"Rosa Daza. She's dead." I hiccup as the tears start.

When Javier doesn't say anything, I lift my gaze to meet his. His glare is frightening. Clenched jaw. Flaring nostrils. Pupils dilated with rage. My tears leak out and race down my cheeks. His hand flinches like he wants to swipe them away, but he doesn't. He can't. Villains must always be villains. Even I know this.

"Dead, huh?" His words are cold.

Michael laughs scornfully, making me flinch from the sound. "She's fucking dead all right. I killed her three and a half years ago."

"What?" I choke out.

He sneers at me. "Six months after we were stationed here, I told them you were raped and killed by some Mexican thugs. Turns out I was a motherfucking fortune teller. Look at you now, Daza."

No longer interested in keeping up pretenses, I take a step forward, my shoulder brushing past Javier. His warmth and scent fill me up. He may be a monster, but he's still a better man than the sick fuck sitting in the chair. "All those meetings. All those recordings. It was for nothing? You let me stay in that house knowing it was all bullshit?"

Angel mutters out a, "Oh fuck, bitch, you're going down."

Marco Antonio cracks his neck loudly from the wall.

"All bullshit," Michael says with a laugh. "And when I got tired of Stokes' whiny ass telling me it was time to close down the investigation and get back, I faked my own death. With a little help, of course. I'd made friends with attorney general Lucas Lorenzo and he paid me really fucking well to do his bidding for him. All he asked was for me to spoon feed my weekly information to him." He shoots me a knowing look that has my gut hollowing out.

"Lorenzo, huh?" Javier asks, coolly. The attorney general will be dead by the end of the week.

Michael nods. "He had the means and connections to keep the agency out of here. The Estrada surveillance was no longer a problem the CIA cared about. El Malo's destruction of this city ultimately funded Lorenzo's corruption, but he still wanted to know your every move. Money works miracles around here. We've been playing this game for years, Daza. A permanent vacation. Acapulco weather, dirty whores during the week, and your fine ass every fucking Saturday."

"You bastard," I spit out at him. "You sick goddamned bastard."

"You were so gullible, sweetheart. Came sniffing around for the dick like a desperate little thing. I couldn't tell you no." He looks past me at Javier. "Your *woman*, Estrada, is nothing but a lying whore who spent the past four years trying to tear you and your entire organization down." Then, Michael looks at my stomach. "Poor you, baby. Won't even get to have that kid. By the looks of the motherfucker behind you, he's going to cut it straight from your body and feed it to you." He laughs in a maniacal way that chills me to my bones.

I turn to face Javier and sure enough, his face has contorted to one of blind rage. He shoves his hands into his pockets and retrieves a pair of leather gloves. With his searing, angry glare on me, he slides the gloves on slowly. I back away from him, completely terrified of the monstrous look on his face I've never seen before. My tears fall harder and I'm unable to stop them. I back right into Angel, who once again grabs onto me in a punishing grip that makes me yelp in pain. My eyes never leave my monster.

My monster.

Despite the hate rolling from him, he's still mine. He'll always be mine.

And I am his.

"Marco Antonio," Javier bellows, the fury emanating from him a living, breathing animal. "What happens when you touch Javier Estrada's girl?"

"You die," Marco Antonio growls.

"Arturo," Javier hisses. "What happens when you touch Javier Estrada's girl?"

"You die," Arturo answers, his voice cold.

"Alejandro," Javier says in a violent whisper. "What happens when you touch Javier Estrada's girl?"

"You die," Alejandro bites out.

"Angel." Javier turns to glare my way, hate dripping from his features. "What happens when you touch Javier Estrada's girl?"

"You die," Angel says, gripping me tighter. He turns to Michael. "He'll cut you open and pull your entrails out. He's fucking psycho."

"You're still claiming her? Knowing what a lying cunt she is?" Michael asks in disgust.

I swipe at my tears and his eyes fall to my shiny ring. Big fat diamond that was ridiculously expensive. My wedding ring.

"You married the whore?" Michael's eyes are wild.

"Javier," I plead. "Please, baby." I want this done. I

want to go home. I want everything to go back to the way it was this morning when Javier woke me up by whispering sweet nothings to our child in my stomach.

Javier's fiery hate isn't on me but on Angel. "She's a lying whore," Javier tells Angel, his voice calm and challenging. "You heard the man. Fucked me over and lied. I married a fucking liar. What should I do?"

Angel laughs, dark and cold. "Fuck her up."

"How?" Javier demands, his jaw tightening.

"We should all fuck her and then hang her upside down from the rafters. Cut her throat and watch her bleed out," Angel offers.

Javier transforms to evil personified as he gestures at him. "Then by all means, Angel. Lead the way." When Javier is in the shed, he likes toying with his victims.

Angel grips a fistful of my hair and I scream, taken by surprise at the forceful way he does it. He pushes me down to my knees. His strong hands rip apart my cotton dress from behind and it falls to the floor at my wrists. Panic, despite knowing it would come to this, overwhelms me. I start to crawl toward Javier, but Angel grabs my hips. My breasts are falling out of my bra as I try to get away. Angel yanks down my panties.

It wasn't supposed to come to this, though. "Javier!" I scream, no longer able to keep up the act. I let out a terrified howl meant for my husband and look up at Javier, but he's gone.

"You stupid cunt," Michael yells, laughing. "You were always so fucking stupid."

From the corner of my eyes, I see Javier circle around. A calm washes over me. I seek out an ally and lock eyes with Marco Antonio, whose face is bright red. He clutches his AK-47 like he's ready to use it.

Lucky for the both of us, he won't have to.

The plan is going accordingly.

"I almost let the information of you feeding secrets to our enemies go because you're nothing but a stupid kid," Javier roars, his voice unlike I've ever heard before. "I could almost look past you roughing up one of my maids because you're still young and don't know how to treat a lady. But every video I watched of you in *my* house touching *my* property like it's fucking *yours...*" He trails off, leaving us all in suspense.

A choked sound resounds from behind me and I scramble away the moment Angel releases me. I cover my chest and back up against the wall. Javier has a piece of metal wire twisted in each hand and is using it to choke Angel. Angel's eyes bug out from his head as his face turns purple, shock gleaming in his frantic gaze. *That's right, asshole. You don't touch an Estrada. Ever.* Blood leaks from where the metal wire cuts into his throat. Javier's face is pure, unfiltered rage as he uses all his strength to yank that wire toward him.

"I tried to give you so many chances," Javier hisses. "I tested you over and over again." He pulls the wire harder. "You failed, motherfucker."

Angel makes choking sounds that turn into gurgling. Blood.

So much blood.

Javier has no doubt sliced through the carotid artery because bright red blood sprays out in a wide arc and splatters the wall. The kid is dead and yet Javier is lost to the madness. He cuts through until he must meet resistance on Angel's spine. With a rage-filled roar, he shoves the body away from him. It hits the floor with a loud thud.

Javier is covered in blood and he's every bit the monster the CIA was after. A killer. A psychopath. An untamable beast.

He's beautiful.

"What. Happens. When. You. Touch. Javier. Estrada's. Girl?" he yells, his face turning purple. His veins on his neck and face bulge with ferocity.

"You die," I breathe out, my voice barely heard.

He snaps his attention my way and stalks over to me. Giant and muscular and scary as hell. And mine.

"You die," he repeats as he drags me into his arms. "*Manzanita*, I'm sorry."

I cling to his blood-soaked apron and tilt my head up to look at him. "I love you, baby."

His features soften and he kisses me sweetly on my lips. "I love you too, *mami*."

Michael lets out a garbled sound. "What the fuck? No. Fucking no. Kill her, you idiot! She's a lying cunt!"

I pull away from Javier and walk over to the tool box. I pick up a hammer before turning to regard Michael. The scent of piss permeates the room as he loses control. Fear has taken over his body. When I start walking toward him, he squirms in the chair.

"R-Remember your place, Agent Daza. As your superior, I order you to stop!" Michael yells.

I pause in front of him, looking down at his pitiful self, the hammer hanging down at my side. Javier's body heat warms me from behind. He grabs my hips and twists me around. His fingers stroke through my hair as he regards me tenderly. My eyes flutter closed when he kisses me, this time harder than the one before. His tongue dances with mine and encourages me.

I am his.

No one is allowed to touch Javier's Rosa Estrada.

No one.

Angel learned the hard way and so will Michael.

"What the fuck, Daza?" Michael hisses behind me. "El Malo?"

I smile against Javier's mouth. My tattoo on my lower back proudly boasts of who I belong to. El Malo. The bad. Javier's good little undercover maid turned cartel and mafia queen.

"Remember, Estrada," Javier says to me, his eyes tender as he regards me. "He hurt you."

I give him a clipped nod.

And then I turn, swinging the hammer violently through the air. It connects with Michael's temple with a sickening sound.

Crunch.

Crunch.

Crunch.

Crunchcrunchcrunchcrunchcrunch.

Over and over and over again I swing my weapon.

Agent Daza is gone.

I am El Malo.

I'm lost to the darkness for seconds, minutes, hours, forever.

Warm, strong arms wrap around my middle and gently pull me away. Someone tugs the hammer from my grip. Another person offers me their black suit jacket. I'm numb as I stare at the now mutilated head of Agent Michael Stiner.

"Why did you fucking make me do that?" I scream at

his unmoving corpse. "Why did you fucking make me do that?" I use his words against him—words he's said to me before—but he doesn't answer.

It's over.

Javier scoops me up in his arms and carries me away from the carnage. We slide into the back of Marco Antonio's Land Rover and he doesn't say a word about the blood we're staining his car with. I cling to Javier as we drive home.

I'm in a daze.

Drifting and drifting and drifting.

I don't start to come out of it until I'm naked with my husband and standing in our massive shower. He dutifully washes me until the water runs clear. And then he holds me. Loud, ugly sobs rip from my chest and I can barely keep from collapsing to the floor.

"Shhh," Javier croons against my hair. "Don't cry, *manzanita*. He deserved it."

"He did deserve it," I agree, choking on my sob. "But she didn't."

His black brows furl together. "Rosa Daza."

"She died. Rosa Daza is dead."

He smiles at me, his dimple forming. "*No, mi amor.* You are wrong. She didn't die," he murmurs as he kisses my forehead. "She was reinvented. Born from the ashes. My sweet Rosa found her fire again and she blazes brighter than any sun in this universe." His palms find my belly. "And she's carrying my whole world."

I thread my fingers with his and nod. "*Te amo,* Sr. Estrada." *I love you, Mr. Estrada.*

"*Yo también te amo, mi dulce y fogosa esposa.*" *I love you too, my sweet, fiery wife.*

Epílogo

Javier

Three years later…

"**M**arco Antonio says the last of the hotels have gone into contract to sell," Arturo tells me. "It is done."

I lean back in my desk chair and kick my feet up on my desk. Sucking in on my candy apple little cigar, I raise an eyebrow in question before letting out a plume of smoke. "Done, huh?"

"*Sí, jefe.*"

Arturo's gaze drifts to the window where Tania and Rosa sit in the shallow end of our new pool. Both pregnant. Both happy. We've only lived in Puerto Vallarta for a year now, but we love it. It's clean and gorgeous. There are even some cliffs worth diving from much to my father's horror.

My father is dancing with Emiliano. The kid is always laughing and playing. Our little María Elena adores her uncle, who is only four years older than her. In her cute little yellow bikini, she wiggles her butt. Her loud giggles can be heard through the glass. God, she's so cute.

"Bring home our boys," I tell Arturo as I stand and snuff out my cigar in an ashtray. He rises and gives me a nod before disappearing to make the call to Marco Antonio and Alejandro.

I quickly stride into my bedroom and change into my trunks. By the time I step outside, Father has María Elena in his arms and she squeals as he spins her around. With my daughter distracted by her grandfather, I dive into the deep end of the pool and swim toward my target.

The sexy Sra. Javier Estrada.

Her belly is big beneath the water. Full with my child. A son this time. Our daughter kept asking the sex, so we found out for her. She's thrilled to have a little brother.

My wife doesn't startle when I wrap my arms around her. She likes danger. I grope her tits for a minute before I surface behind her.

"Hey, handsome," she greets, a smile in her voice.

"Hello, beautiful."

She relaxes against me and I rest my chin on her head. My thoughts drift to the night when she told me she was pregnant with María Elena.

"I took a test last week and another to be sure this morning, but, Javi, we're going to have a baby," she tells me, her smile widening.

I toss the test and the cigar to the floor before grabbing her hips, yanking her to me. My lips crash to hers and I kiss her until she's moaning against my mouth. Gripping her by the ass, I lift her and walk her to the very wall I intend on fucking her against. Except when I make it there, I don't move. Simply press her back to the wall and stare at her.

"¿*Voy a ser papá?*" I will be a daddy?

She nods, tears welling in her eyes. "*Sí.*"

I maul her, eager to show her just how happy I am when she palms my scruffy cheeks. Her eyes are sad and serious. "You don't doubt my love do you?"

"*Nunca más.*" Never again.

"*Bien.*" Good.

She pulls me closer so her lips brush against my ear. I'm drunk on her news, but her whispered words sober me up.

"I'm tired of lying."

"Lying?" I growl.

She clings to me. "Just listen, Estrada. Don't talk. Listen."

Fuck, she's fierce. My sweet Rosa.

"I'm not who you think I am," she admits. "My real name is Rosa Daza."

I pin her with a severe glare. Her walls are down. She's finally letting me in. I fucking told Arturo and Marco Antonio to give her time. Rosa is strong and fearless. Braver than most men. Plus, she loves danger. And what her lips are letting slip out are very dangerous words.

"My father is David Daza. A criminal. A bad one." Her nostrils flare. "Like you, baby."

I arch a challenging brow at her, but she doesn't waver. Whatever it is she's saying, she won't stop now. Pride surges through me at her bravery.

"He went to prison for his crimes and left my mother all alone to take care of me. She loved him. When I was younger, I didn't get it. I didn't understand how she could love a monster."

Her fingers tenderly stroke through my hair. "But I understand now."

Tears well in her eyes as she remembers her mother, but she doesn't stop. She continues, lifting her chin. "Criminals like my father shot up the restaurant we were visiting. My mother was a casualty. From that moment on, I decided I wanted to avenge her death by going after every Mexican mafia monster I could. I studied hard in school. I remained focused. Eventually, I was accepted into the Central Intelligence Agency."

"Rosa—"

"I said be quiet," she bites out, her brown eyes flaring. I have this woman in my arms blabbing her most hidden secrets that could affect whether she lives or dies tonight, and still, she's fearless. "Four years ago, I was assigned under my superior, Michael Stiner, to go deep undercover. The agency wanted me to infiltrate Javier Estrada's organization. I was to spy and learn everything I could from the inside while Michael gathered intel from the outside." She frowns. "I worked so hard. So diligently. I hated you and everything you stood for."

A growl of warning rumbles through me, but she's not fazed by it.

"But then…things changed. You looked past the maid façade and saw Rosa. Your interest was piqued, and to be frank, the moment you took notice, I wasn't immune to your charm. I fell hard for you, Estrada. So damn hard."

I should kill her.

A smart criminal would.

He'd snap her neck and toss her body over the balcony.

Avoid all the heat she could bring down upon me if she chose to.

But, apparently, I love danger too.

"And now?" I ask, my voice husky.

216

She draws my head closer to her, our lips nearly touching. "And now, I'm yours. I think I was that night when you looked after me in the kitchen. That's when I awoke from the fog I'd been drifting along in. Everything was so clear and I finally felt alive."

"Rosa Daza," I murmur, trying out her name aloud, but certainly not the first time. "I know."

Her brows furl together in confusion. "What?"

"It took some digging, but Arturo finds people. He started sniffing you out the day you put the smackdown on Julio. Marco Antonio was just sure you were a professional. Turns out, he was right. At first I was angry, but you were so goddamned brave. Prancing around for years in the Estrada house, sneaking information. And, truth be told, I needed to be sure before I did anything. Before I dragged your pretty ass and ended you in the shed, I needed to know if the things that were happening between us were real. By the time they had information on you, I was in love, manzanita. I kept waiting for you to bring down the hammer and it never came. At that shop, I was just sure you were going to call in reinforcements and everything between us would have been a lie."

"We were never a lie," she breathes, her voice firm and fierce.

"But I had to be sure." I rest my forehead against hers. "I had to be sure."

"I know."

"Rosa?"

"I'm sorry, Javi."

"I know, mami."

"Are you going to kill me now?" She tilts her head and regards me.

"Never, manzanita. You're mine."

She smiles. "I had to be sure."
"I know."

"You're quiet," she murmurs as she turns in my arms to face me. Her huge belly separates us, but I don't mind. It's pretty fucking cool when my son kicks me for getting too close to his mother. "Everything okay?"

"Just thinking about you."

She grins, her smile blinding me with her beauty. "Funny, I was thinking about you too."

"Good or bad?" I tease as I kiss her plump lips.

"Always bad." She nips at my bottom lip and it makes my cock jolt in my trunks. "You're Puerto Vallarta's newest and most terrifying villain after all. King Baddie."

My palms slide to her ass and I squeeze her. "And what does that make you since you're married to me?"

"The bad wife?"

I chuckle as I admire this woman.

My woman.

"You're a good wife, *mami*. So good."

She clutches my balls under my cock through my trunks and flashes me a devilish grin. "I guess I better start working on baddie skills." Her hand squeezes me to the point of pain, causing a growl to rumble through me.

"Careful there, *manzanita*," I warn. "You're dancing with danger."

"Well, I do love to dance," she teases. Her eyes darken as her red lips quirk up on one side. "And we both know I *love* danger."

Fin

(The End)

Playlist

Listen on Spotify

"Let You Down" by NF
"Bad At Love" by Halsey
"Love On The Brain" by Rihanna
"The Night We Met" by Lord Huron
"Him & I" by G-Eazy and Halsey
"Havana" by Camila Cabello
"Dark Side" by Bishop Briggs
"Blood In The Cut" by K. Flay
"I Found" by Amber Run
"Picturing Love" by July Talk
"Bad Things" by Machine Gun Kelly and Camila Cabello
"Lips Of An Angel" by Hinder
"Lights Down Low" by MAX and gnash
"Can I be Him" by James Arthur
"Duele El Corazon" by Enrique Iglesias
"Sour Times" by Portishead
"Back To Black" by Amy Winehouse
"Drowning" by Banks
"Hatefuck" by Cruel Youth
"I Do What I Love" by Ellie Goulding
"Wicked Game" by Stone Sour
"Mad Hatter" by Melanie Martinez
"Weather" by A Story Told

"Something I Can Never Have" by Nine Inch Nails

"The Fire" by Bishop Briggs

"Woman" by Diana Gordon

"Cocaine Cinderella" by Jutes

"Issues" by Julia Michaels

"If You Want Love" by NF

"Silence" by Marshmello and Khalid

"Wolves" by Selena Gomez and Marshmello

"Desire" by Meg Myers

"I Really Want You To Hate Me" by Meg Myers

"Homemade Dynamite" by Lorde, Khalid, Post Malone, and SZA

"Monsters" by Ruelle

"Love On The Brain" by Cold War Kids and Bishop Briggs

"River" by Eminem and Ed Sheeran

"do re mi" by Blackbear

"Sorry" by Halsey

"I Feel Like I'm Drowning" by Two Feet

"Love Is a Bitch" by Two Feet

"Lil Darlin" by ZZ Ward and The O' My's

"Young Dumb & Broke" by Khalid

"Despacito" by Luis Fonsi and Daddy Yankee

"Felices los 4" by Maluma

"Never Be the Same" by Camila Cabello

"A Change Is Gonna Come" by Greta Van Fleet

"Meet On The Ledge" by Greta Van Fleet

"Figures" by Jessie Reyez

Books by
K WEBSTER

2 Lovers Series:
Text 2 Lovers (Book 1)
Hate 2 Lovers (Book 2)
Thieves 2 Lovers (Book 3)

Alpha & Omega Duet:
Alpha & Omega (Book 1)
Omega & Love (Book 2)

Pretty Little Dolls Series:
Pretty Stolen Dolls (Book 1)
Pretty Lost Dolls (Book 2)
Pretty New Doll (Book 3)
Pretty Broken Dolls (Book 4)

The V Games Series:
Vlad (Book 1)

Taboo Treats:
Bad Bad Bad
Easton
Crybaby
Lawn Boys
Malfeasance
Renner's Rules

Carina Press Books:
Ex-Rated Attraction
Mr. Blakely

Four Fathers Books:
Pearson

Standalone Novels:

Apartment 2B

Love and Law

Moth to a Flame

Erased

The Road Back to Us

Surviving Harley

Give Me Yesterday

Running Free

Dirty Ugly Toy

Zeke's Eden

Sweet Jayne

Untimely You

Mad Sea

Whispers and the Roars

Schooled by a Senior

B-Sides and Rarities

Blue Hill Blood by Elizabeth Gray

Notice

The Wild – BANNED (only sold on K Webster's website)

The Day She Cried

My Torin

El Malo

Acknowledgements

Thank you to my husband. You're my hero and protector. I love you more than I could ever truly express.

A huge thank you to my Krazy for K Webster's Books reader group. You all are insanely supportive and I can't thank you enough.

A gigantic thank you to my betas who read this story. Elizabeth Clinton, Ella Stewart, Misty Walker, Amanda Söderlund, Tammy McGowan, Jessica V. Viteri, Shannon Martin, Amy Bosica, Holly Sparks, and Rosa Saucedo. You all helped make this story even better. Your feedback and early reading is important to this entire process and I can't thank you enough.

A giant thank you to Misty Walker for reading this story along the way and encouraging me!

Rosa Saucedo, thanks for cheering me on and feeding me inspirational songs for my playlist! I hope the Rosa in the story made the real Rosa proud!

Thank you to Jillian Ruize, Gina Behrends, and Nikki Ash for proofreading this book and being such supportive friends. Your eagle eyes are amazing!! You ladies rock!!

A huge thank you to Nany Vazquez, Mr. Vazquez, and Dora Ruiz Davalos for your Spanish translations! I can't thank you all enough! Gracias!

A huge shout out to my sister Holly Sparks! You're an awesome lady, a great supporter, and a whiz when it comes to keeping me organized. I appreciate and love you!

A big thank you to my author friends who have given me your friendship and your support. You have no idea how much that means to me.

Thank you to all of my blogger friends both big and small that go above and beyond to always share my stuff. You all rock! #AllBlogsMatter

Emily A. Lawrence, thank you SO much for editing this book. You're a rock star and I can't thank you enough! Love you!

Thank you Stacey Blake for being amazing as always when formatting my books and in general. I love you! I love you! I love you!

A big thanks to my PR gal, Nicole Blanchard. You are fabulous at what you do and keep me on track!

Lastly but certainly not least of all, thank you to all of the wonderful readers out there who are willing to hear my story and enjoy my characters like I do. It means the world to me!

About

K WEBSTER

K Webster is the *USA Today* bestselling author of over fifty romance books in many different genres including contemporary romance, historical romance, paranormal romance, dark romance, romantic suspense, taboo romance, and erotic romance. When not spending time with her hilarious and handsome husband and two adorable children, she's active on social media connecting with her readers.

Her other passions besides writing include reading and graphic design. K can always be found in front of her computer chasing her next idea and taking action. She looks forward to the day when she will see one of her titles on the big screen.

Join K Webster's newsletter to receive a couple of updates a month on new releases and exclusive content. To join, all you need to do is go here (www.authorkwebster.com).

Facebook:
www.facebook.com/authorkwebster

Blog:
authorkwebster.wordpress.com

Twitter:
twitter.com/KristiWebster

Email:
kristi@authorkwebster.com

Goodreads:
www.goodreads.com/user/show/10439773-k-webster

Instagram:
instagram.com/kristiwebster